Off-Court

A Steamy Sports Romance

S.C. PRINCIPALE

Table of Contents

Dedications and Acknowledgements

To all the single parents out there who are worried about falling in love again... I hope you find the perfect fit the second time around.

To all the people who suddenly find themselves in the "seasoned romance" category... what the heck? Since when is that 'thirty and up'? Okay, well, just remember... we're seasoned. We taste better. ;)

Lastly, thank you to Judy, Rachelle, Sofia, LoLo, Terry, Judy I., Grace, Mikayla, Michelle, Dawn, and my massive long list of writing support sisters.

Introduction

Ray "The Rocket" Robinson was a college All-Star and a shoe-in for the NBA, but when he came down wrong on a trick play, his dreams shattered right alongside his ankle. Brynn O'Dell was the women's high scorer in her NCAA division.

That was twenty years ago. Now, two old stars missing their glory days are pumping their dreams into the next generation (literally) by coaching their teenage daughters' basketball teams. When an end of season game goes bad, these two decide that a game of one-on-one is in order to settle the dispute. But when things get hot and heavy, will two passionate players decide to take their battle off-court and into the bedroom?

Chapter One

Ray put on his black and white jersey and listened to the roar of the crowd. Any minute now they would cheer "Rocket, Rocket, Rocket!"

"Rocket! Rocket!" The sounds warped and blurred in Ray's head. Game Mode Engaged. That's what his old high school coach called it, that moment when you start to psych yourself up and everything else fades out.

"Rocket! Rocket!"

That would be his cue to step on to the hardwood and let everyone know that Ray "the Rocket" Robinson was going to save the day. He never missed a free throw. He had been flirting with numbers like Stephen Curry for three-pointers. Not to mention every cheerleader on that team would gladly give him some encouragement before or after the game to keep him looking fresh for the NBA scouts flocking the front row of the bleachers.

"Dad! Dad, Can Samantha and I go get ice cream after the game?"

Poof. Ray "The Rocket" Robinson turned back into regular old Coach Robinson, thirty-five, divorced, and coaching his only daughter's Junior High basketball team. The cheers of "Rocket, Rocket!" were not for him. They were for Raquel "The Rocket" Robinson, or as he sometimes thought of her, "Rocket, Second Stage." Okay, so they were probably for the team... the Ryndell Rockets, but still, his baby was definitely one of the star players. He couldn't be prouder. And if he was a little wistful, a little lost in his memories, so what?

"Earth to Daddy! Ice cream? Samantha? After the game?"

"Uh, sure, sweetie. Probably. Who's Samantha? We don't have a Samantha on our team, do we?" Ray looked at his roster, suddenly worried that his ankle hadn't been the only thing messed up when he'd been fouled during a tricky jump shot sixteen years ago. Was he getting forgetful before forty?

"Samantha's a Shark, not a Rocket."

"A St. Stephen's Shark? You're fraternizing with the enemy?"

"Da-a-ad." The way Raquel drew out the single syllable word into a triple break told him that even though his daughter was fourteen, she was still his little girl and not above whining and pouting to get her way.

"Well, you'll have to ask Samantha's parents."

"It's the last game of the season, and it's a Saturday. I'm sure her mother will say yes. She's super nice. I had a summer basketball clinic with her at the community center, remember?"

"I don't know," he said with mock gravity. "Don't those Catholic kids have to get up awfully early for Sunday mass?"

Raquel rolled her eyes. They have mass like seven times a day at St. Stephen's, Daddy. Besides, Samantha and I said we wanted to get one ice cream cone, not stay up all night binging like you and your old college team used to do."

"Hey, my basketball team was a group of dedicated and serious athletes. We were in bed by 9:00 every night unless we were studying to keep our GPAs up." Ray hoped that Raquel wouldn't notice that he crossed his fingers under the clipboard.

This time, Raquel didn't even have to say a word. Her rolling eyes gave him all the sass he could handle. Why did his baby girl have to be as pretty as his ex, but the miniature version of him? All attitude, argument, and A-game?

"Fine, sweetie. Concentrate on the game. Point the kid out to me when the game is done, and I'll ask her parents."

Raquel jumped up and kissed his cheek, balancing on the tiptoes of her white and pink high-tops to do so. "You're the best, Dad! Don't worry, I'm going to win this season. The Rocket legacy lives on." She pumped her fist and huddled up with the other girls waiting just beyond the locker room doors.

***

"Show no mercy. You're a Shark. This is your last chance for a good meal. Who's hungry for some Rocket fuel?" Brynn smiled teasingly at her group of players. St. Stephen's was a small school, but they spent a lot of money on their athletic department. Brynn's daughter had the best coach money could procure—namely, her.

"What about love and mercy, Mrs. Donovan?" One of the girls asked, nervously fingering the gold cross that hung around her neck.

"Love and mercy are wonderful values, Kaylee, but save them for off-court." Brynn O'Dell Donovan winked when she said it, hoping the girls wouldn't go back and complain to the Mother Superior that Coach Donovan was acting a little *too* much like a shark, the team's starving apex predator namesake.

So what if she was? It had been fifteen years since she had turned down an offer to play in the WNBA when she realized that most players would make more as head coaches. Of course, most players hadn't been four months pregnant at the time and planning to get married the next weekend.

Samantha hurried over to her, an elastic band in her outstretched hand. "Mom! Quick, can you put my hair up in a bun? I'm really hot."

"You sure are sweetie, you're on fire. You're breaking the scoring record tonight." Brynn tucked her clipboard under her arm and pulled her daughter's long hair through the band with a practiced snap.

"If I win, can I go out for ice cream with Raquel?"

"Raquel? Isn't she on the other team?"

"Yes, but that doesn't matter, does it? Even if they lose, she'll still want to come. Raquel is *so* nice. She lives in our neighborhood, but she goes to the public school. We see each other at the bus stop every day, but we never really talked until we were both in the summer clinic at the community center. You know? *That* Raquel?"

Brynn did recall Sammi getting to be immediate friends with a tall, slender girl with long, intricately braided hair and an incredible jumpshot.

"It's okay with me. Did she ask her mom?" Brynn quickly wrapped Samantha's long red-gold hair into a bun and secured it to the top of her head with the elastic band and a bobby pin that she fished out of her coach's windbreaker pocket.

Samantha made a shushing noise. "Don't be so old-fashioned. Not everyone has a mom and a dad."

"Oh." Brynn shifted uncomfortably, wondering just how old and uncool she had become since she turned into a stay-at-home-mom, followed by a working-single-mom. A working, single mom who does nothing but watch basketball and coach her daughter's team, she thought ruefully. "Did Raquel ask her dads?"

"Just the one. She said she'd ask him. She does have a mom, but she says her mom lives in Arizona and doesn't stay in touch. She was a cheerleader on her dad's college team. They eloped and got divorced when Raquel was only like—two." Samantha turned to her with wide eyes. "We could be twins! Except we look nothing alike, and my dad left and her mom left, and—"

"Okay, okay, baby. I get it." Brynn put a soothing hand on Samantha's shoulders. Her daughter was practically vibrating with nerves.

"Grandma says Raquel's mom and my dad were 'not the marrying kind.'"

Brynn choked on a gasp, eyes closing in mental anguish. "Oh God. Don't bring up Grandma right now." Somewhere in the stands, her mother was wearing a St. Stephen's Sharks jersey and had sprayed her whitish hair blue and gold with wash out dye for the final game of the season.

"But I love Grandma!"

"I know, Sammi, I know, but not now." Brynn gave her daughter a little shove to scoot her back to the rest of the team so she could clear her head of all the thoughts Sammi had just dumped in it, the top thought being a comparison of Brynn to her mother. Her mom had the knack for remaining effortlessly cool, no matter what life threw at her. Brynn wished she had gotten the cool, feisty rebel gene instead of the obsessive compulsive perfectionist gene.

"But then, I wouldn't be an awesome coach, and my girls wouldn't be about to win this year's final game."

Chapter Two

"It's a tie! 107 and 107 in double-overtime! Congrats to the Rockets and the Sharks!"

Ray had already been pacing the team seats in the paint, but at the tired-looking referee's announcement, he exploded onto the court. Across the way, a tall woman, almost as tall as him, was marching over, her eyes ablaze and her nostrils flared. Good. Back up, Ray thought. All night, he and the Shark's coach had been at odds on every call, but now they were united.

"You can't call a tie! This is the final game of the season!" Ray shouted.

"These girls have worked way too hard for this!" The Shark's coach, Brynn Donovan, he believed, stared down the ref, her dark, coppery red braid whipping around her head in her fury.

"The youth league rules stipulate that no game may exceed a double-overtime or two hours, whichever comes first. Your girls don't seem to mind." The ref calmly blew his whistle and the scoreboard buzzed and flashed before the words Final Score blazed across the top. Home: 107, Visitor: 107.

The crowds erupted in a different way, their screams long and high-pitched in glee. Sharks and Rockets piled onto the center court, high-fiving, hugging, and fist-bumping. Parents were swarming out of the stands, ordering the girls to go pose in front of the now-frozen scoreboard.

"What? What?" Ray was so mad that he couldn't articulate. He wanted to scream a few choice swear words, but not in front of this nun-lady.

"Damn that damn youth league stipulation!" Donovan raged, and clamped her teeth together, sucking in enraged breaths.

"That bastard."

"He didn't make a good call all night!"

"I wouldn't say that. He was clearly a Shark's fan," Ray scoffed.

"Excuse me? He benched my Samantha twice!"

"He's the a-hole who made me threaten legal action about Raquel's hairstyle last year."

"What a piece of—"

"Sweetie! What an amazing game! What excellent sportsmanship!"

"Raymond! My granddaughter deserves a triple-scoop! Where are we getting this ice cream?"

Ray turned to see Raquel, glowing with pride and sweat, hanging on a miniature version of the angry nun-lady and flanked by his mother and another lady of similar vintage and wild taste in hairstyles.

"Uhh..."

"Samantha. Introduce me to your friends?" The old woman with blue and gold hair and face paint demanded as she seized a package of tissues from her purse and began to scrub at her face.

"Grandma, Mom, this is Raquel Robinson and Nana Robinson."

"Call me Vi."

"And this is my dad. Dad, this is Sammi and her grandma, Catherine. You already know Mrs. Donovan."

Ray shook hands and plastered on a smile, seeing his mother's gimlet eye boring through him, clearly checking to see if he was still the decent, mannerly boy she had raised.

"Group photos! Let's get Sharks, then Rockets, and then all the players together! Coaches come on!"

"Vi, I bet the coaches will need to be here for a bit longer, and the parking lot is a zoo! After the photo-op, would you and Raquel like to come with us to Sundae Drive for an ice cream feast?"

"I surely would! Raymond, will you and Mrs. Donovan meet us there?"

"Yes, Mom. Right away."

"Mom, I don't want to put you to any trouble," Coach Donovan protested, but her mother cut her off with one well-placed look. "Let me get my purse."

"Nonsense. It's my treat for Sammi!"

"And mine to Raquel!" Vi chimed in, daring him to argue.

He had failed at every argument that night. Ray put his hands up, kissed his daughter, and smiled. "Let's go take pictures, babe. Good job, Li'l Rocket. You, too, Sammi."

"Thanks, Mr. Robinson! You're a great coach. Oh, you, too, Mom."

Brynn Donovan looked as crappy as he felt.

***

Being a coach wasn't as glamorous as being a player, Brynn groused silently, wiping off the folding chairs and stacking them. Later, she would send out the obligatory group email thanking all the parents for their support—pretending to forget about how Terry Gingary's mother was always ten minutes late picking up her daughter and ignoring the fact that Belle Eddleston had not once volunteered to be snack mom or substitute assistant coach. Then, she would have to get team and individual awards ready for the end of season sports banquet in two weeks.

A clatter and curse across the gym distracted her. "Man!" Ray Robinson was collecting the dozen balls that had just escaped from his equipment bag.

Brynn stacked the final chair and hurried to catch the balls bouncing her way. "I thought you were already gone."

"Almost. Would've been. Zipper broke. Um, hey—" Ray stuck his hand out and left it out. "I'm sorry I was kind of a jerk earlier. I hate tie games."

"Me, too!" Brynn shook his hand. "I'm Brynn Donovan."

"Sammi's a natural."

For some reason, Brynn had never liked that term. It denoted a blessing of talent absent of hard work—at least in her head. "Thank you. She works hard. She practices every night."

"Yeah? So does Raquel."

Was this some kind of parental or coaching one-upmanship? Brynn gave him a tight smile. "Well, she's got a fabulous hook shot."

"I taught her that. I used to play. D-I."

"Cool. Me, too. D-I."

"I mean in Division One college basketball. The NCAA," Ray spoke slowly.

Brynn eyed him, trying to keep her face neutral, even though words like "chauvinistic, gatekeeper, and jerk" were starting a worrying spiral through her brain and down to her mouth. "Yes. I know. I know, because I played in Division I College Basketball, too. Only my team had less chest hair and less television coverage."

"You? Back in the day?" A look of new respect and surprise passed over Ray's face.

Words like *cocky bastard* were edged out by other thoughts. *Handsome.*

No, not handsome! Do not notice that!

"You probably didn't watch any girl's teams. I—"

"Now, back up. I watched plenty. I'm a big WNBA fan, too! I want my daughter to have the same shot a son would have had. I can't recall any Donovans, that's all."

"Brynn O'Dell. I played for—"

"Chicago! Loyola? Girl, I had a low-key crush on you," Ray chuckled and slapped his hands together. "No way! I can't believe that."

Brynn blushed. "What? Oh, wow. That's... flattering."

"You probably don't remember Ray 'The Rocket' Robinson. I might have been before your time. I kept my butt on the bench most of my senior year." Bitterness flashed across his features. "I didn't make it to the pros after that. I had a bad break. A freak break."

Brynn nodded. Robinson hadn't been on her radar, but she vaguely remembered the news of a freak fracture during a major game. "You needed surgery to avoid a joint replacement, right?"

"Right, but the first surgery was unsuccessful and they had to break it again. Then they put six pins in it. My career was over before it ever really got started. I had to scramble to come up with a new plan, and of course, I met Jayla."

"Your wife?"

"Ex-wife. She was a cheerleader for the team. We looked good together. Made a beautiful baby girl together, but—" Ray rocked his head from side to side, weighing his words, "she was taking a calculated risk. She got me when I felt like I needed to cling to the basketball world and she expected me to get back into it. When she became a professional cheerleader and I switched to math education, it got messy."

"That's why you have Raquel full-time? Sammi mentioned her mother lives in Arizona."

"She's a choreographer for the Cardinals now. Travels a lot."

The lights suddenly flickered off overhead. Brynn gasped and then tried to laugh it off. "I guess we've been here too long. The custodian must be heading out. Do you have everything?"

"I'm good to go. I'll see you at the ice cream place."

"Right." Brynn gathered her things and walked to the large double doors of the St. Stephen's gym. They opened onto the parking lot. "It was nice to get to talk to another nethead. Most of the coaches I meet are parents—nothing wrong with that! But sometimes I take it more seriously than they do, and they all look at me like I have three heads," Brynn laughed, tucking her braid over her ear. And it was also nice to talk to a single, handsome man who liked kids, was an educator, and liked basketball. She didn't often get to meet men in her line of work unless they were colleagues or the fathers of the students.

"Do you still play? You know, in a pick-up league or anything?"

"Hm? Oh." Brynn had been so lost in her own thoughts that she wasn't aware of Ray talking at first. "Oh! No. I can't. If I'm not teaching health or coaching, I've got Sammi. Her dad isn't around."

They walked to their cars, which were parked several spots apart in the row closest to the building. "Great minds," Brynn chuckled, trying to keep the conversation going for a minute while she figured out what this strange feeling was. She hadn't felt it in such a long time. Was it... interest? Attraction? Curiosity? "Coaches are always lugging everything around. It makes sense to park close."

"Yeah."

Brynn paused in the act of putting her purse in the front seat. There was a strange, drawn out quality to his answer.

"It's a shame they ended this in a tie. Not for the girls so much, but I think you and I wanted a clear victory. Some time you and Sammi should meet us at the Ryndell playground after school. We could have a game of two-on-two. Or one-on-one. Show the youngsters how it's done."

"I'd like that." Brynn nodded. When she got behind the wheel, her heart was fluttering. Yes. This was curiosity and interest. She had no idea if Ray Robinson was interested in her as anything but a person to shoot hoops with, but even the idea of making a new friend, a friend who would fit into her busy life of coaching and single-parenting, made her smile.

Chapter Three

"Dad!"

"Mom!"

Ice cream-smeared faces beamed at Ray as he held the door of the ice cream shop for Brynn.

"Girls! Hi, champs!"

"What's up, ladies?"

"Dad, Sammi's grandma is taking her to the Pumpkin Hollow Craft Show next weekend. Can I go?"

"Honey, I don't know. You can't just—"

"Raymond, I'll take her. You might have other plans you should attend to." Mrs. Robinson's voice was light and sweet, but her eyes were all too pointed.

Ray nodded quickly and gave his daughter a big smile. "I'm going to join you two in a victory scoop. I'll be right back." He was not going to let his mother do this to him again.

Vi Robinson had long ago decided that her son could dunk, shoot, dribble, and even teach pre-algebra. What he could not do was land a good woman.

Ray had to admit that his mother had proof of this. He had gone through high school basketball groupies and cheerleaders like a kid diving into Halloween candy after it's been checked by a parent. He'd always done the breaking up, too, usually because he'd realized the girl was into basketball and being with a basketball *player*, not him.

And then of course, there was the great big undeniable proof—his ex-wife. The very definition of fickle. She'd loved him when he was about to go NBA and dumped him as soon as she was positive that those dreams were shot to hell.

Post-divorce? Well, that was even worse. At first, he had met a lot of women who wanted a cute toddler girl and *he* was the gift-with-purchase. Then, he met a lot of women who wanted him, a good-looking, "sensitive guy" who taught kids—who bolted when they found out he had sole custody.

Dating with a pre-teen? Not likely. Dating with a teenager? Oh, Lord. No.

His mother's sing-song voice was suddenly right beside him, although about a foot-and-a-half closer to the ground. "Raaay-mond. Hey there, Coach. Good job tonight—even if you did make a fool of yourself after the final buzzer with that poor referee."

"Thanks, Mom." Ray had long ago learned that the less he argued with his mother, the better—at least about most things.

"I love Raquel's little friend. And Catherine O'Dell! Why, we've lived in the same town for over a decade now and somehow never met. That woman is an angel. You could do worse for an in-law."

Ray almost cursed at the freckle-faced teen waiting to take his order. "Mama! Uh, sorry. Two scoops of peanut butter chocolate chunk, please." Ray scooted down the counter to wait his turn. "Mama, don't say things like that. Brynn Donovan and I don't even know one another."

"I know." His mother gave him a pleased smile. "That's why I'm gonna take Raquel with me next weekend so you can take Brynn Donovan out to dinner."

"No. Mom, no. Stop now."

"The girls get along. You're both teachers. You both coach. You were both D-I. Did you know she was D-I at Loyola?"

"Two scoops of peanut butter chunk."

Ray took his cone in relief. "You could say that about 9000 other people in the country, probably. Doesn't mean we mix. Now drop it."

His mother said nothing, which meant she wouldn't drop it unless she felt like it.

Ray returned to their table and scooted in beside his daughter. "That looks good, Daddy. What'd you get?"

"Peanut butter chocolate chunk."

"Oh, hey, that's Mom's favorite." Sammi beamed up at him, chocolate on her nose.

"How about that?"

"Mom, did you know Raquel's dad played D-I, too?"

Across the table, Ray locked eyes with Brynn, trying to smile in a polite, friendly way.

Damn. All of the sudden, at just that angle (he was sure it was just that angle, and the lighting, or maybe because he was so tired) Brynn looked incredibly gorgeous. High cheekbones. Big green eyes. Red hair. She had a long, slender body, like his, but of course, she also had— Ray jerked himself to a halt before his eyes could go surveying the rest of Brynn's assets.

"I did hear that, sweetie. We're two old pros. We're going to have to have a pick-up game sometime. Robinson versus Donovan."

"It sounds like a boxing match," Catherine O'Dell hooted. "Watch out, Coach Ray. My daughter may look like a lovely lady, but she's a wildcat."

"Mother!" Brynn looked mortified.

"Oh, good. Your mother says embarrassing things, too." Ray rolled his eyes in commiseration.

"Always." Her cheek dimpled when she gave him an exasperated smile.

"It didn't stop when we left the nest, huh?"

"It might have gotten worse when kids came along."

There was laughing, laughing all around, and he relaxed. Brynn Donovan could become a good friend. They could swap babysitting and coaching tips. They could comfort each other during the ordeal of teaching teenagers to drive, or swap horror stories when Sammi and Raquel discovered the evils of teenage boys.

But damn if Brynn wasn't even prettier when she laughed.

***

"Thank you for a great season, coach!" Brynn stuck out her hand as she climbed back into her car. Sammi, Raquel, Vi, and her mother were still gabbing and plotting next weekend's outing.

"Yeah. Yeah, it seems a shame to wait another year to start up."

Brynn waited. There were basketball clinics and other rec leagues. She had a feeling there was something else Ray wanted to say about basketball. Or maybe not about basketball.

"Were you serious about wanting a pickup game?" Ray leaned against his car, then put his weight on his other leg, shifting as if preparing to defend the net.

Brynn knew that kind of restless energy. All the girls on her old teams had long since stopped playing. It was like being a mom or even a woman with a job suddenly sucked any passion for sports out of you—not. Maybe it was simply society's expectation that women shouldn't make time for themselves, their friends, and their hobbies, especially not if she were so unlucky as to be a divorced, single mom. Before she could think of anything besides the fun of playing a real game, not just coaching one, or demonstrating the same skill over and over during a clinic, she blurted, "Yeah! I'd love to. We—We could settle that double-over-time, right?"

"Sure. But honestly... I was just thinking that I'd love to play with you. I mean, play with you, another old pro. Not old! Oh, shit."

Brynn laughed. Ray Robinson was probably about her age, but he had the look of a naughty boy caught with his hand in the cookie jar when he fumbled his words. "I know what you mean. I'd love to take on the legendary Rocket."

"Don't flatter me."

"I'm not! You know all the players on the girls' teams wished for a shot to take one of the pros!"

Take one of the pros.

"Well... I'm not gonna lie, sometimes I'd check out a WNBA or Women's NCAA game and wonder if I could go deep enough against those girls. Like you! Man, you could take it to the hole like no one else on your team!"

Brynn hoped the darkness would hide her suddenly bright cheeks.

Take it deep.

To the hole.

All of the basketball slang suddenly turned dirty and her brain belonged to a curious seventeen-year-old again.

"Maybe while the moms and kids are away, we can play?"

Yep. Even that sounded dirty.

She suddenly wondered what it would be like to get him alone, really alone, off-court. "Would you like to come over on Saturday?"

"Absolutely. Best two out of three?"

"You're on."

Chapter Four

"We'll be back by bedtime. You and that nice Brynn Donovan are having lunch this afternoon?"

Ray stood in the kitchen of his rancher, watching his mother pack enough food for twelve people into a cooler. "They don't have food in Pumpkin Land?"

"Raymond."

"That was tonight's bedtime, right? Or did you mean bedtime a week from Christmas?"

"*Raymond.*"

He stopped teasing his mother, leaning over and kissing her plump cheek. "We'll grab a bite, but mainly we're meeting up to play some one-on-one." Ray stopped and shook his head. "It's been over a decade since I played with a real baller." His old college ball friends were scattered and hadn't bothered to keep in touch. The few (very few) who made it past those golden doors into the NBA had never looked back. He wasn't in the "lifestyle." Even if he'd accepted those decades' old, half-hearted offers to "get together some weekend," his weekends normally meant braids, not beers, and grades, not babes.

Brynn Donovan was a bit of a babe.

Actually... way beyond a little bit. She had those legs that went on forever, and this impish grin, and... and so what if he'd happened to go through his old copies of Net Magazine and stare at her picture for way too long?

An icepack shoved into the middle of his chest startled him back to reality. "Huh? Ow, Mama."

"Ray, do not blow this. That's a nice, solid, sweet-tempered woman. She has a good job. She has roots. She has a brain, a daughter, and her mother is a hoot! Most importantly, Raquel likes her. You wanna be single forever?"

"Mom, c'mon. It's one game. It's not even a date."

"It could be if you worked a little harder. Do you want to be old and alone? Do you want to wait until you have dentures to date again?"

He stared at her in sheer horror. "Mother. *Stop*."

"I'm perfectly serious, Raymond. You're in the prime of your life right now. This is your last chance to marry someone who can help you raise your daughter and finally give that little girl a sister."

Ray shut the freezer and steered his mother to a chair in his kitchen. "Oh-kay. Mom, did you have a stroke on the way over? I don't think the blood is flowing to your brain right now." A light slap reminded him that his mother didn't accept sass from anyone. "I think you're rushing into things." *Rushing* me *into things. No, not rushing, going warp speed.*

"I only seem to be rushing because you're used to moving like a blind turtle in quicksand!"

"Nana!" Raquel came barreling into the kitchen, long legs propelling her like an overexcited jackrabbit. "Can we go yet? Sammi texted me. She's ready to go." His daughter's big brown eyes settled on him and scanned him with appraising eyes. Ray braced for the usual comments about how uncool his clothes were.

"Sammi's mom is cute. And she's smart, too. Are you wearing that to meet her?"

Ray looked down at a faded Rockets tee and plain black shorts. "Well, I'd look kind of stupid playing ball in a suit, sweetie. I don't care how 'cute' or smart her mom is, she's an old-school baller, too." Raquel burst into giggles, which she smothered under her hand. Ray glared. "Real mature. I wish you two would get it into your heads that this is just a game between two coaches. If I was playing the coach of the Union Jr. High Lancers you wouldn't be carrying on this way. Now, get." He shooed them toward the front door. "You both go buy a ton of little things to clutter up the windowsills and hang on the walls."

His mother and daughter came over and hugged him. He felt like the luckiest man in the world during these moments, with such good women in his life—the best mother in the world and a daughter anyone would be proud of.

He didn't usually feel a little nugget of emptiness.

There should be a third woman here. A wife, a sweetheart, something.

"Daddy's really stubborn, isn't it?" Raquel pulled out of his arms and hefted the cooler.

His mother joined her, grabbing the other side. "He sure is, baby."

"Mrs. Donovan can be kind of scary. I've seen her yell."

"Well, good." His mother tossed him a final smug look as she exited the kitchen, "sometimes people need a good scare."

***

"Mom, is this a *date*-date or like a play-date?"

Brynn finished braiding her hair while Sammi paced by the bedroom window, waiting for the distinctive sound of her grandmother's rattling old Chrysler. "A play-date, I guess."

"You haven't dated anyone since Daddy?"

Brynn pushed away thoughts of the dozens of first dates she'd been on over the years, most of which had been half-hearted set-up attempts made by friends or her mother. "No. I haven't. This isn't a date, honey. You have nothing to worry about. Me playing a game of one-on-one with another coach is just like you playing one-on-one with a good friend on your team."

Sammi came over and put her arms around her mother's middle, ducking Brynn's elbows as they weaved and tucked the long red strands of hair. "I'm not worried about you dating someone nice, like Raquel's dad. I might go off to college in a few years."

Brynn huffed out a laugh, "You'd better go to college in a few years, young lady!"

"No, Mom, I mean I might go *off* to college. Away. You could be all alone. You and Grandma. You would turn into two little old ladies, with purple hair and knitting."

"Okay, one, unless your grandma gets sick, she's staying in her own house. We lived together for eighteen years, and that was plenty. Two, no matter what you do to my hair, I don't think you can make it purple."

"Mo-om." Sammi broke the word in half with a groan. "You know what I mean. Raquel and I were texting. We think you two should try going out together. You have a lot in common. He's cute. You're cute. You're both single—"

"No matchmaking. There are a ton of reasons why Mr. Robinson and I could never be anything more than friends."

Sammi's face fell. "There are? Why?"

Brynn paused. Why was her daughter so insistent?

Oh, yeah. I raised her that way.

"I don't know that we believe the same things. You know, about religion and stuff." Catholicism. That good old guilty excuse.

"You might. Grandma says people from different faiths can get married."

"Married? Married! Samantha, stop using the m-word."

"She also said you were single, technically, because you had the marriage... disintegrated?" Sammi's eyes scrunched up.

"Dissolved. It's the Catholic church's way of torturing you a little bit extra while you're getting a divorce."

"See? You know church stuff isn't perfect."

"Don't say that at school."

"I will if I want. It's called freedom of speech."

Brynn put her hands to her cheeks and groaned. "It's called a sit-down with the principal."

"You don't even have to be Catholic to teach at my school, or go there. You know that."

"I do know that, but it helps." Brynn heard the rattle-sputter-wheeze of her mother's car easing into the driveway. Saved by the transmission. "Come on, enough silly talk. Are you excited to go spend the day with Grandma and your friend?"

"Yes!" Sammi hugged her hard before darting off. "Love you, Mom! I'll let Grandma in."

"Oh, no! No, I'll walk you to the car." The last thing she needed was her mother joining this bizarre conversation.

***

It was Sammi's fault. Sammi put questionable thoughts in her head. Brynn used her absent daughter as a scapegoat and completely ignored the fact that last night's conversation over ice cream had piqued her interest in Ray Robinson. Ray Robinson, who was striding up to her across the empty outdoor ball-court, the very definition of tall, dark, and oh yes—stupidly handsome.

Some men age like milk. Some men age like wine. Ray was definitely in the *pinot noir* category.

"Girls got off okay?"

"Yeah! Hi. Oh! Hi." Brynn stumbled over her greeting as she reached out to do the obligatory coaches' handshake, but at the last second it seemed to morph into a hug hello, like greeting other school-pal moms at those mind-numbing PTA meetings.

At least Ray seemed as awkward as she was, not knowing whether to hug or handshake. The basketball that had been tucked under his arm was somehow transferred into her hands during their exchange. "Oops."

"Well. That must be a sign. Play ball." Brynn tossed her hoodie on a bench and grinned. He smiled back, broad jaw exposing a dazzling smile that made her chest compress.

"Sounds good."

***

This felt like the good old days. No, better. In the "old days" he hadn't even known what a relief it would be just to take an hour or so off from his hectic life and do nothing but try to score on someone.

His young college self would definitely have been trying to score *with* someone, too. Brynn Donovan was an effing beast on the court, and he wanted to find out if she was the same way off-court.

He blamed his mother. She put those bad, bad thoughts in his head.

"Two out of three," Brynn reminded him as they paused, greedily gulping water. "Should we make this one more than twenty-one points?"

"Then we'd have to do all of them over, wouldn't we? My endurance level would give me the edge on a longer game."

"Endurance level? Ha."

"Oh, what's that smack talk?" he laughed, capping his bottle and heading back to the concrete court.

Brynn swung her braid over her shoulder, fixing him with her green cat eyes, sparkling in the sun. "In my experience, women have way more stamina."

"You played against some weak-ass men."

"You played against some pretty princesses. I can go as long as you. Longer."

His cock jerked suddenly, and he told it to sit down and shut up. "Fine. Best two out of three, starting now. 45 points."

"You're on. The first two were just warm ups."

"Yep, just to get things loose."

She smirked, just for a second. Did that sweet-tempered "good girl" have a dirty mind?

Damn. Now his cock would need a sedative to go back to sleep. His imagination filled with far too many scenarios about repressed Catholic school teachers who were wildcats in bed.

Unprofessional. Impolite. Not okay.

Was that any way to think about this nice, responsible pillar of the community?

"Well, I don't know about you, but it's been a long, *long* time for me."

Ray's mouth practically watered as he kept track of the ball, trying to concentrate. Of course he'd seen some questionable videos when he was a college boy. That was always the line of the desperate housewife. *It's been a long time. I'm starved for attention.* "Oh? How long?"

"Oh, not since before Sammi was born."

"What?" He let her score on him, shocked out of step. "How long have you been divorced?"

"Divorced? About ten years. But that has nothing to do with it. My husband didn't play. To be honest, he didn't even husband."

"Dickhead."

"Exactly."

"But why would my divorce—"

In sheer desperation to avoid explaining how he'd taken her innocent remarks and turned them filthy in his head, he fouled, stole the ball, and ran it up the court.

Brynn was right after him, coming behind him with an eagle's shriek."Oh, you wanna play dirty? I can *get* dirty!"

Ray groaned as she stepped across him, grinding her hips back into his to cut between him and the ball. He just couldn't get a break.

***

"Oww." Brynn limped to the table at Rosa's, the Mexican taqueria they'd chosen for lunch.

"I'll see your 'ow' and raise you a 'damn' and an 'I'm an idiot.'"

"You have an excuse. Your ankle." She was being generous. They had played a total of four complete games, two where they'd each racked up a 21-point victory, and then two where they'd each managed to scrape out a 45-point win. About fifteen points into the third (or fifth) game, her muscles had begun to scream. Ray had started favoring one side. They'd given each other a mercy killing at twenty points, with no clear winner.

"We're going to have to settle this some other way."

"Or another game of one-on-one next week. One game. Sudden death overtime. All the glory." Ray winced and pulled a chair over, pushing his swollen ankle on top of it.

"Here." Brynn drained her Coke. She put her empty glass, still full of ice, against his ankle.

"Thanks."

"Don't mention it."

"No, seriously, thank you. This was so much fun." Ray chuckled, a dark, smoky chuckle that made her skin tingle. "So much pain now, but so much fun, then."

She pushed the tingle away. "I know! You have to take time for yourself. All the psychologists and television gurus say it, but parents don't do it."

"Not single parents, that's for damn sure."

"Amen to that." They clinked glasses together.

"So... Question?"

"Ask away." She bit into her taco, realizing that if she had wanted to seem sexy and alluring, she should have suggested coffee, not a food that tried to fall apart as you ate it. She also shouldn't be sitting in sweat-soaked clothes with her braid in a billion wisps.

"You haven't played basketball since before Sammi was born?" Ray looked at her with wide, pitying eyes.

"No. I was still playing low-key games with some of the girls at the community center, but then I had a scare and ended up in the ER. Baby and I weren't getting enough oxygen when I was playing, so I stopped. Then, after Sammi was born, my husband was clueless and refused to learn how to take care of her, so I didn't go out and get back into a community league. Then he left, and..." Brynn shrugged. "I've played a random game here and there. I tried joining a league a couple of times, but life got in the way. The first time, our car died, and I didn't have a ride, plus I needed to save all the favors of asking for rides for things like getting to work and doctor's appointments. The next time—chicken pox, followed by a double ear infection, followed by strep. I missed the first three practices of the season and I figured God was telling me that it wasn't my year."

"What about now? Now that Sammi is older and your wheels work?" Ray asked, dipping chips in salsa.

"You're a coach. You tell me."

"Yeah, I hear you. Every night is their practice, not ours."

"But this is great! Just one-on-one."

Ray nodded, swallowing hurriedly. "I was thinking that we should make it a regular thing—although not if you're going to be so savage on me."

"You ain't seen nothing yet." Wait, what did she mean by that? She had given it her best. She had definitely shown Ray every ounce of skill that her mid-thirties-muscles would allow.

Maybe being around him made other savage instincts pop up in the back of her mind?

"I've tried to organize a few things with other dads from the team. Someone always has to cancel and back out, and then it's a domino effect. But if it's just two people—"

"It's much more convenient to schedule. And we can get the girls in on it."

"They seem to adore each other."

"I'm glad. Sammi's so shy," Brynn confided.

Ray shook his head. "I wish Raquel were a little more shy! She's so outgoing. I'm afraid one day I'll find her 'outgoing' with a boy I didn't even know about!"

"They're good for each other."

"Mmhmm, a nice balance."

They took a break from conversing to eat. Brynn stopped worrying about her hair. Her body hadn't burned that many calories in such a short space of time in years.

It was nice to carb-load with another athlete.

"Two more?" Ray asked as he reached the bottom of his basket.

"I'll get them, you rest your ankle."

"Thanks, babe."

Ooh. Babe? She hurried away, cheeks pink again. She knew she was blushing, but it was probably just a slip of a tongue. Or maybe not even. He might have been trying to say 'Brynn' with a mouth full of salsa.

"They were out of the carne asada so I got the carnitas." Brynn returned from the taqueria's buffet station with two loaded baskets.

"All good." Ray toyed with his straw, stirring the ice in his red plastic glass before he said, "You and Sammi should come over sometime. I make a mean carne asada. Aaaand—we have a hoop and decent-sized driveway...well, if people park on the street."

Is that a date? No, it's a play-date. The kids were invited. But... is that what dating is like when you both have kids?

Does it matter? Do you want to see him again? "How's next Sunday?"

Chapter Five

"Mmm-mmm-*mmmm*!" Ray swiveled his hips and salsa-stepped in place.

"You're a dork, Dad. You dance while you cook."

"All the great chefs dance while they cook."

"They do not. I've never seen Bobby Flay dance while he cooks."

"You need to watch his early stuff," Ray teased his daughter and started halving avocados. "Raquel, can you— whoa. Whoa, whoa, no way. What are you wearing? We're going to play some two-on-two after dinner!" Ray turned around to see his daughter, his sweet baby girl—looking like a miniature version of her mother in a tight white and black dress, strappy flats, and lipstick. Lipstick! "Wipe that off! What are you doing?"

"Sammi and I are going out with Miss Catherine and Nana. Surprise!" Raquel tittered with a nervous smile, tucking a strand of hair behind her ear.

"What? Who... no one told..." Ray sputtered so much that he almost sliced off the tip of his thumb as well as cutting the avocado in half.

"Nana said you and Mrs. Donovan make us spend every weekend in shorts and jerseys. They're taking us to the theater and dinner at a fancy French place."

"Well, I'll just be calling Nana about that." Ray yanked his phone off the counter. "You love spending your life in sneakers and jerseys, don't you, baby?"

Nothing.

"Don't you?" That uncomfortable, ice-trickling-down-his-neck-into-his-insides feeling of failure assaulted him as Raquel didn't meet his eyes. Just like when the doctors had stood looking over his x-rays back in college, one thought kept hammering into his head. *I screwed up.*

"Raquel."

"Yes... mostly! Daddy, I never get to dress up and go anywhere fancy. I know you probably don't like me doing my hair in new styles and wearing lots of make-up because it reminds you of my mother—"

"Shit," Ray muttered. Psychology strikes again. When had his little peanut turned into a smart, grown-ass girl?

Raquel continued, "I like being fancy sometimes. I want to go somewhere with napkins folded like swans and see the big red velvet curtains open up on a stage. Nana says... Nana says you don't want me to grow up, but I *have* to grow up. It doesn't mean I'll stop loving tacos and basketball. I just want... I just want tacos and high tops, and high heels and champagne."

"Champagne?" Ray's voice was a low, sonic boom.

"Not actual alcohol! You know what I mean. I want to be everything. You told me girls can do it all. I want to be a girly girl sometimes and a total terror on the court other times. Is... Is that okay?" She bit her lip and looked up at him, twisting her hands.

That look always melted him, but it melted him a little extra right now. His little girl was turning into a young woman, and instead of helping her navigate the wider world of womanhood, he'd been scared. He'd tried to keep her safely tucked on the sporty side where he knew how to help her. "I bet Sammi's grandma and Nana can help you with the... the fancy dresses. When you need them. But you're not dating and you're not drinking champagne. I put my dorky Dad-foot down about that!"

***

"Those four are menaces." Brynn showed up at his house with a bottle of wine and a bottle of sparkling grape juice. She was wearing jeans and an untucked white button down shirt. Her hair was unbound, flowing in an ocean of autumn-red waves down her back.

Hell. She looks gorgeous. She doesn't have makeup on, no jewelry, no heels... Why? How is that fair? It threw him, completely different from the accessory-obsessed women he'd preferred in college.

"I got your text about the 'ambush' just as Raquel gave me a heart attack." Ray stepped back and let her in, wondering if he'd been staring for a creepily long time.

"Oh?"

"I turned around from the stove and she was there—looking like she was about twenty. With lipstick!"

Brynn laughed gently. "Nothing so bad about a little lippy."

"Let's just say it causes flashbacks to my ex. And I know cheerleading is a serious competitive sport... to some. But it seems like a shit-ton of makeup is part of the uniform."

"Ah. Well, my ex would have approved of that. He didn't like that I was a tomboy." Brynn rolled her eyes and leaned against the kitchen island.

Ray tried to keep his mouth shut. He failed. "Nothing wrong with that, either."

"We met at a Loyola banquet. I was dressed up. He was in a tux. I got an award for something, he got me drunk... I traveled a lot for D-I games, and he always made a big deal about me coming back to campus. Very superficial, but since I'd never had a boyfriend," Brynn shrugged and twisted one long strand around her finger, "I thought as long as he kept wanting to take me out to nice restaurants and buy me roses, we were doing it right."

Ray put homemade guac and chips next to her. *Tacos at a greasy buffet while your puffy, pin-filled ankle sits next to her? Then you have her here to do what? Listen to the dishwasher running and then play ball in your driveway?*

She definitely doesn't think this is a date. Your head is as hard as the hardwood, Ray.

"Sorry. I shouldn't have brought him up."

"I brought mine up first. Here, you open that wine and I'll get the glasses. Let's drink a toast. To the fools who left—may they stay the hell away."

Brynn tossed her head back with a sudden burst of laughter. "Ooh, I like that."

"What kind of wine is that?"

"Cheap."

He laughed at that. "Ohh, pinot noir."

"Apparently my knowledge of wine pairings is... nonexistent. So I hope that's okay? We could stick to the sparkling juice. I brought that for the girls so they could feel 'grown up.' Believe me, I know all about what you're going through with Raquel. Sammi's getting insecure about being on the thin, flat side. It's my fault. I cursed her with my genes."

Ray looked down at her jeans as they took an inaugural sip of sweet, dark wine together. Ray knew Brynn meant the genetics that created her long, lean body, but it didn't take a genius to see that the years had added small, sweet curves to her frame. "I think your genes look great. Sammi's lucky. And so's Raquel. Here, a second toast. To our beautiful girls."

"To our beautiful girls."

***

"Mom says they should be back around ten. I don't want to impose on you that long." Brynn pushed her phone back in her pocket and finished her second glass of wine. How had she gone through two before the meal? She didn't even drink. A pleasant, warm glow was seeping through her, fueling her imagination.

This could be life someday. Our girls out together at the mall or a dance. Our moms at some function. Wine and dinner for two with a nice man.

A nice man? Seriously, are my standards that low?

Yes. Yes, they are, but that doesn't mean Ray is at that level.

Another forty minutes in Ray's company, inside his home, had raised her opinion of the man quite a bit. She could tell that he'd been a family man first and foremost for a long time, but she liked seeing touches of his life as a basketball star woven in.

"You're no imposition, believe me. You'd better not strand me here with enough carne asada to feed those two piranhas they call teenage girls."

Brynn laughed at that, hurrying to help take things to the table. She laughed a lot in his company, but she couldn't help it. The humor was real and relatable. "I know! How do they do it? Every year my Christmas bonus goes to shoes and frozen waffles. I swear she eats an eight-pack every other day."

"At least frozen waffles have some nutritional content. Raquel eats that fake-fruit cereal. She must go through four boxes a week. I can't even stop her by refusing to buy it at the store. She'll go to the corner gas station and buy a box for three times the price. Do I teach her to budget or let her eat fifteen kinds of food coloring?" Ray groaned. "At least it's not popsicles. Hell, at least she eats. I complain, but with the girls I see starving themselves—"

"It's an epidemic at the junior high level!" Brynn agreed, slamming down a plate of warm tortillas. "Oops. Sorry."

"Nah, girl. Go on and get mad."

The warm glow burned hotter. Her first (and last) relationship had been carefully constructed and balanced, right up until the end. With Ray... Well, it wasn't a relationship and she was just herself, and damn if that didn't feel pretty amazing. Pretty freeing. She poured them each another half-glass of wine, finishing the bottle. "Don't get me started on the way they're sexualizing the clothes, even the school uniforms!"

She was off—and he was going with her.

***

How was it eight? How was it eight at night, pitch black, and they were still sitting at the table, picking at remnants of the sweetly spicy grilled beef? "Have I really been here for so long?" Brynn looked at him with surprise. "Did that sound rude? My filter is off. I didn't mean it to be rude. I'm so... relaxed around you. I'm having fun." Fun (non-mom fun) was an almost forgotten sensation.

"Unfiltered Brynn is fun. I think it's a little late—and I'm a little full—to take you on one-on-one."

"Oh. Yeah." The bright, slightly tipsy bubble she was riding began to lose air. "Well, thank you so much, Ray. You're a fantastic cook. We'd love to have you and—"

"Wait a minute, wait a minute." Ray hopped off his chair and made a beeline for a shelf in the dining room. "I still gotta beat you in something basketball-related."

Brynn watched him stretch and pull a board game off the high shelf. His untucked t-shirt rode up, revealing taut abs and the hint of black ink spiraling over his ribs, continuing to a hidden picture on his back.

Bad boy.

Okay, no, tattoos didn't make you bad or good, but...

Bad boy. Her pleasantly lubricated brain couldn't help compare the only other male body she had intimate knowledge of—blank and smooth, like his personality. Tame until pushed, and then unkind and absent. Ray made her think of rockets in more ways than one. Sparks. Fire. Flights into the unknown.

Ray turned and plopped the box in front of her. "Net-ivia. It's basketball trivia. I bet you I win."

"I bet you don't." She gave him a saucy smile, leaning back in her chair to look up at him. Tall. Handsome. Tattooed. Damn it, she needed to calm down. She was starting to let her brain go beyond dating to "serious relationship" stuff. *Physical* stuff.

"Yeah? You're on."

"What do I get if I win?" She asked the question before she could think about what his answer (or hers) might be.

Ray gave her a long look, sitting across from her and prying the lid off the box. "What'd you have in mind?"

Brynn quickly reached in and started pulling out the tiny plastic scoring chips and markers that accompanied the game. "N-nothing. I was being silly."

"I know—the winner gets an instant ten-point lead the next time we play one-on-one."

"Ten points! That's a huge lead."

"That's nothing for Brynn O'Dell," Ray teased, shaking out the rule book. "Besides, no one has ever beaten me at this game, so that ten-point advantage is going to be mine." He flashed a smug smile at her.

Brynn perched on the edge of her chair, brain waking up. "I have a thing for shattering the grandiose illusions of men. I don't get to do it every day, now that I'm divorced."

"Ha." Ray's laugh burst out, short and sharp. "I hate to deprive you of the pleasure, but I'll make up for it with chocolate cake. Coffee with dessert and a side of defeat?"

"Coffee and cake—hold the gloating."

Chapter Six

It wasn't fair, and he should be pissed about it.

For the third time in their recent history, neither one could best the other. They racked up points evenly. Within five minutes, Ray had abandoned the game and was just plowing through the trivia cards, quizzing her with half the stack of cards while she quizzed him with the other. He and Brynn questioned each other relentlessly, but neither of them slipped.

Well, not at answering. In his thoughts? Oh, yeah. He had that caveman urge to grunt, reach over, and grab Brynn by the shoulders, pulling her onto the table in order to kiss her into submission. Bet you I can win at that, his pouting brain muttered.

"When I couldn't play because I had a newborn strapped to my chest around the clock, I read every book of basketball trivia written."

"Same, only instead of a newborn on my chest, I had a broken ankle on my leg. I thought I was storing up tidbits for my retirement and natural progression to ESPN commentator," Ray chuckled, ending with a melancholy sigh. "At least I'm the teacher who always has a sports trivia of the day question on the board. The kids love that."

"I bet they do. I bet they love you in general. I wish my high school math teacher had been sweet and funny. I had Sister Bernice Elizabeth, and she was famous for keeping you after school to re-do an entire test if you got more than one question wrong."

"Yikes. That would never fly in a public school."

"Things are changing at St. Stephen's. Things are sort of... changing in general. Maybe I'm having a midl-life crisis."

"Not unless you're about ten years older than me, girl."

"No, no. But suddenly... I'm thinking of doing things. New things, daring things. New people."

He knew it was an innocent slip of the tongue, but his brain had left innocent behind when she named all the original NBA teams in ten seconds flat. "Doing new people?"

Instead of being offended, she squeaked and giggled, looking up at him, green eyes daring him to tease her again. "Any person would be a new person for me. I was only ever with my ex."

Ray wanted to shout, "What? Really?" but his common sense saved his ass at the last second. If anyone asked him how long it had been since he got laid?

It would be embarrassing to say the least.

"Dating is hard with kids." Brynn drew herself up in her chair, wounded defensiveness cloaking her like an oversized hoodie.

"Tell me about it. But... I've been feeling daring, too. Especially around you." Ray stretched his hand across the table and let his thumb stroke the back of her hand. "I know you don't want to rush into anything." He remembered that his mother and daughter really liked Brynn. That he really liked her, as a colleague and a coach. AS a friend. He told his animal lusts to simmer down and wait. A kiss would be a good start.

Brynn was silent. She wound her fingers through his and squeezed. At the same time, under the table, one of her long legs tangled through his, and his thighs jumped in excitement.

Oh.

"I definitely don't want to rush... but it's eight-thirty, and if I want to be sitting on my couch at home by ten..."

"Oh! Yes, definitely."

Brynn rose. "I haven't—"

"I got you. Like a team this time, not rivals." Ray hurried to her side of the table, adrenaline spiking. Remember. Slow. Soft. Gentle.

Brynn turned to him, letting her lips meet his.

And any thoughts of slow and soft went out the window.

"Bedroom?" she panted after her first burning, needy kiss threatened to set him on fire.

"This way."

***

He couldn't think in full sentences, but Ray decided he was okay with that. One thought kept thudding into his mind, along with the pulsing of his cock. Brynn was a natural. The college commentators had always said so.

She was a natural beauty, shedding her clothes in the dimness of his bedroom. He had a small desk lamp on, but the rest of the room was dark.

"It's been a long time and… I don't want to be like I was. I was very—passive."

"You can boss me around any day, baby." Ray watched as her bra dropped to the ground, revealing perfect, round breasts. He was mesmerized by the gentle slopes that fit her narrow torso, the pale, moon-white of her skin, and oh… oh God. Black cotton panties snapped off to reveal a narrow strip of bright fluff.

Yes. Every rotten little teenage fantasy he had about gingers came back.

"I don't want to boss you around. I just want to…" Brynn paused, swaying up to him, and running her hands down his broad, smooth chest. "I want to be like I am on-court, even when I'm off-court."

"A fucking goddess? A powerhouse? A natural?"

"Not scared. Willing to take risks, take long shots, and oooh. Or other long things." Her hand found its way into his boxers and stroked up and down his hungry shaft. It bucked in her hand, and she did that adorable squealing giggle of surprise again. "He likes me."

"Sweetie, any man with balls and brains would like you."

"I like that you have both." Brynn felt around for the aforementioned equipment. "Condom?"

"Somewhere. I'll find it."

"Can we wait a little bit?"

"You call the shots."

"Hmm. Okay. *This* time. But next time, you can. Get those shorts off, Rocket-Man."

He was in heaven.

***

She was in heaven. Even though she hadn't asked for it (she wouldn't have known how to ask for it), Ray was insisting on "eating her sweet peaches before we get to the cream." For a second, she hadn't been sure if that was what it sounded like.

It was.

Brynn found herself shaking, writhing as Ray buried his head between her thighs, his hand also doing things she'd never known possible. The best part? He was explaining it all while talking to her in that low, velvety voice that made her drip.

"Guys might freak out if they knew, but your clit had a shaft, just like a cock. DId you know that?" His thumb and forefinger squeezed her mound, right where her soft patch of fluff was. Instantly, her clit throbbed. Ray continued while she wheezed out a moan. "This is where all the action is. Just like when you stroke a guy, he should stroke you. He shouldn't just be sucking on that pretty little bead—even though it's adorable and I get why men forget you gotta give mo—hang on." He paused, kissing her clit, but then sucked the entire top of her mound into his mouth, using his head to bob against her, pulling on the hidden tissue that she had previously been unaware of. Well, sort of. She knew it was there, but no one had ever done much with it.

"So," Ray lifted his head and grinned at her, "you gotta work the whole thing. And then, none of this one finger in jabbity-jab. Two fingers, deep, slow, rock, and roll." Two of his long, strong fingers entered her and pushed in deep. With firm rocking strokes, he moved from side to side, in and out.

It was electric. It was like—her cheeks flamed, but then blood traveled south—it was like two men at once, one penetrating her, one eating her out. Her walls fluttered and spasmed, and before she knew it, she had come on him. Really come, not a polite burst of pleasure to pander to his ego.

"Your turn."

"You get three licks of this lollipop," Ray said sternly. "More than that and we're going to have to make this a double-header."

"I'm in favor of that. Hell, let's make it a series."

"Mmm, Brynn. Baby, you're amazing.

She felt amazing. She felt like the goddess he claimed her to be. With a sultry wiggle, Brynn sat up, tossing her hair back and prowling down to his cock with a trail of kisses.

I'm a bad girl. A wild girl. And that's just perfect. Terror on the court, or off.

She dove, devouring him.

***

Ray growled as his wild cat sucked him without a pause. Her hands were around him, her lips sucked him, tongue flicked him. He would have used the word sloppy, but all of her movement had a grace in their frenzy.

"Put that pussy on me," he groaned when she was about to burst him, and damned if she didn't climb aboard, sinking her tight, wet sheath over him, wincing a little as she swiveled her hips to take all of his above-average length. "Easy." He said it for two reasons. One, she was rusty. Two, he might pop in two seconds.

"Oh my God! This is why women get big toys at the adult shop," Brynn moaned, lost in her own pleasure.

Ray laughed with her. "Big, huh? You sure it's not just because you've got the tightest little pussy?"

"Maybe we're a good combo."

"Mmhmm, good team."

He watched as she bounced slowly on him, not speaking. Concentration crossed her face, then pleasure. When her jaw went slack, he pulled her forward, gripping her forearms as she dug her short nails into his shoulders. He hammered his hips up as she bore down, and he watched that stiff, sweet, good girl come all over his cock, cursing and kissing him.

The best part? He wasn't done.

He didn't bother with the condom, deciding instead to pull out. He couldn't have forced himself out of her snug, hot nest right then anyway, not when he was going to give her a proper fucking, one like only the Rocket could dish out, one that her ex would never have dreamed of. Balls deep with this beauty on her back, his hand on her clit, making her pulse and come over and over until he shot across her belly.

That was how he visualized the game.

And even after all these years... visualizing the win still worked.

"You good?" he asked, kissing her shoulder as he came down next to her.

"I never... sex was never like that." Brynn gave him a wide-eyed, winded look.

"But was it *good*?"

She slapped his arm before pulling him into a long, lingering kiss. "Next time, we're going to do this at *my* place. I want the home court advantage."

Chapter Seven

"Hi, Mom. Ray and I were going to get together this weekend. Do you think Sammi and Raquel might like to do something with you and Mrs. Robinson?" Brynn sat on her bed, her portable phone propped under her chin as she painted her toenails. She hadn't painted them since she and Sammi went to the beach a few years ago. Funny how Ray had started their relationship (if you can call it that) while they were wearing the most unflattering clothes possible—puffy track pants that crinkled when you walked and t-shirts, and that their first "date" had consisted of tacos and leg cramps. He'd found her sexy as she was, and now Brynn felt a renewed confidence swirling back into her life.

Her mother poked at it. "What are you two doing together? Sammi said you've been texting him all week."

"He's a new friend, Mom! I text my other friends, too." But she didn't text them dirty innuendos and talk in whispers on the phone until one in the morning, her hand between her legs as Ray described exactly what he'd like to do to her the next time they were alone.

"Hmm. I like the idea of you and Ray. But what about Sammi? What about work?"

"What about work? What about Sammi?" Brynn put down the pale pink paint and ignored the buzz from her cell phone. Ray was texting her. He always texted her before bed, even if he was swamped with grading.

"It's nothing. It's nothing, really."

"Mother. If it was nothing, would you have mentioned it?"

"Well, you teach at St. Stephen's. He works for a rival school. You're Catholic. He isn't. Your marriage was dissolved by the church once you provided enough proof of abandonment and adultery. What about him? Is he willing to get an annulment?"

Brynn bit her lip, stomach knotting. Her mother hadn't pushed her into marriage—exactly. But trying to live up to her mother's rigid expectations had led her to make some hasty choices. When she'd found out she was pregnant with Sammi, she'd hurried into marriage. When she'd suspected her ex was using his travels as an excuse to sleep with other women, she'd kept quiet, because divorce was frowned upon. When he'd left and they'd gotten a divorce, the dissolution had been another big hurdle. "Mom, I don't even know if Ray and I want to go on a date." Mentally, she changed that to "a third date." Did this count as their second or third date? Did they count the first post-game ice cream?

"Well, Vi and Raquel say he's smitten with you and you have to think about these things now, before your hearts get involved."

Is my heart involved? No. No, of course not. We're just having fun. Right? "We're just friends." *Friends who have insanely good sex. A friend I shaved my legs for. A friend I shaved something else for.* Brynn blushed and squirmed on the bed.

"You're thinking about being more than his friend right now, aren't you?" her mother accused.

Brynn flopped back. "I don't know! Would that be so bad? You were pushing me along, you and Sammi."

"No, it would be wonderful... but you have to think ahead. Don't let your heart run the show."

Brynn sighed and nodded. "Yes, Mother. What about Saturday afternoon? Would you like to take Sammi and Raquel out shopping for their Spring Formal dresses? I'll give you the money."

"Ooh! I would love to! Let me call Vi and see if she wants to. We could make a night of it, you know. The girls could stay at my place. I could slice cucumbers and show them how to use mudpacks. We could watch old movies like *Sixteen Candles* or *The Golden Girls.*"

"Sounds like a blast, Mom."

Brynn hung up and abandoned her toes. Her stomach was going to keep her up unless she settled her nerves. She wanted to vent her fears and worries to someone, but the only one who might actually make her feel better or have any answers was Ray.

"You can't talk to him about this!" she hissed to herself, turning off the bedside light. "Men hate when you get serious fast. He thought he was dating Brynn O'Dell, fun D-I dinosaur."

Her phone buzzed. The buzzing turned to a ring. Ray must want to do more than text. "Hello?"

"How's my gorgeous angel of the nets?"

Honesty snuck right out. She was too rusty at dating to have her armor on and her excuses ready. "Sucky. My mom called and freaked me out."

"Is she skipping out on babysitting? Well, Brynn, don't worry about that. We can take the girls out to a movie or something. You can hold onto the home court advantage until another weekend." Ray's voice was low and comforting, with no guilt or pressure.

It undid her careful reserve. "If we get serious, she's worried it will affect my job, and the church will have something to say about your divorce. Not to mention where would we live and would your daughter like me as a stepmom, and... and feel free to panic and not see me again. I was going along all happy, shaving my coochie and painting my toenails, feeling like I was sexy again, and now I feel like a divorced, single parent with a triple decker burger of guilt."

Ray was silent—she thought. The silence turned into a snuffling, huffing sound, which turned into laughter. "I'm not laughing at you, Brynn. Girl, we're parents! We're coaches! We're teachers, for fuck's sake. We are planners and worriers. Of course, those thoughts were bound to creep in. My mother was already talking about me dying alone if I didn't make a move when God popped a nice, sweet woman in my path. Look, I'm not the running kind. Not when I care about someone. And I... Well, it hasn't been long, but I care about you."

"In the stories, the hero and the heroine always say that they'll find a way if they care enough. But it doesn't always work like that, does it?"

She wiped her eyes with a single knuckle. It was stupid to cry, but her tearducts didn't seem to remember the rules. Brynn Donovan had to be tough and self-reliant, there for her students and her daughter, there for her widowed mother and her teammates.

"Not always, baby. But... But we can give that old fairytale a rewrite, can't we? If two old ballers like us refuse to be beaten, then we won't be beaten. Come on. You know we're unstoppable. I'm still trying to beat you, but I can't. The second you curl up against me, I'm out like a light."

"Oh, Ray." Brynn rolled onto her side, heart lifting slightly. "I was afraid to talk to you about this, but you knew just what to say."

"Well, that's a first. My ex-wife *and* my mother would tell you that! You're just easy to talk to. Um." Ray laughed, a hesitant, self-conscious sound in her ear. "You're the first woman I've ever treated like this. Not that I treated them badly, or that I was selfish... Okay, I was probably selfish. I wasn't sure how to treat women, and I didn't think they wanted the same things I did, that's for damn sure. I don't feel that way now, and I don't feel that way about you. You think it's because we're older and wiser?" he mused. "Or because you're so irresistible and such a badass, and I'm still so cool?"

She laughed. Ray always made her laugh. "I'll err on the side of tact and say both. So, now that you've calmed me down... do you want to rev me up?"

"I thought you'd never ask."

***

Ray lay on his back, panting. He hadn't done this since... ever. Phone sex wasn't a thing when he was in college, at least not for him, as he cherrypicked his way through cheerleaders and hoop groupies. He'd heard some of his teammates calling their girls back home when they were traveling across the country. Ray had thought they'd been fools, settling for voices describing carnal acts instead of sticking it to whatever willing pussy was available. When he'd finally gotten serious with Jayla, his traveling days were done.

"You're so amazing." Ray found enough air and brain cells to pay a compliment to the redhead on the phone. He imagined her splayed out, still rubbing her soft, shaved snatch. Yes, he knew she'd shaved, just for him, and he was going to eat her like the pretty peach she was, and then give her every inch of his cock, in at least three positions.

And then he'd need a nap.

"What are you thinking about?" she asked with a soft laugh.

"That I wish I'd met you when I could go for six hours on a bag of chips."

"Hate to tell you, loverboy, but we're parents. If we got six hours alone, three of them would have to involve running an errand, making a phone call, or sleeping."

"That's what I love about you. You're real. You're the real deal, Brynn, and I think..." Ray swallowed. He hadn't felt like this in so long. In ever? No, never. He'd never felt this mixture of friendship, companionship, admiration, and desire. "I think I'm really crazy about you. I'm going to show you how much on Saturday."

***

"Mom, is Ray going to spend the night here?"

Brynn spit her coffee into the sink. "What?" she gasped, whirling to face her daughter. The answer was—she didn't know.

"Well, we're staying overnight at Grandma's. Is it so you two can..." Sammi became fascinated with her waffles, pouring syrup neatly into every single square. "Be alone?"

"Honey, that's so you can have fun with a friend and so Grandma and Mrs. Robinson can have fun, too. Finding a good friend when you're a teenager, or a senior citizen, or even a busy adult, is a big gift."

"Oh. So you and Ray are just friends? Nothing romantic?"

Brynn could avoid, but she didn't want to outright lie. "I would like there to be something romantic if Ray feels the same. Have you thought that this might be something serious? Not now, but someday? It could mean you'd have to share me, or share our house. You'd have—"

"A dad who plays basketball and actually knows how to braid hair? Who cooks and comes to my practices? A sister? Two grandmas in the same town? Yes, duh, Mom. I've thought of it. And if it's not the greatest... I'm almost an adult."

"Oh, please don't say that," Brynn groaned softly, eyes closed as she sipped her coffee.

"But it's true. If you find someone when I'm a grown up, that should make me happy. Because you'll finally be at that point where I won't need you every day. Not physically! Mom, don't cry. Oh, Mom!"

"I'm supposed to be the old, wise person in the house," Brynn sniffled, hugging Sammi tightly.

"You are. I'm just the young, wise person. You raised me right, as Nana Vi would say."

"Nana Vi, huh? Do you like her?"

"She's awesome. I think she might even make a good mother-in-law. Just saying."

"Samantha Donovan!" Brynn gasped, but under her pretend shock, she felt quite comforted by the fact that her daughter was so mature, and that Ray's mother seemed to like her.

Now. How did she really feel about Ray? Wasn't it too soon to tell? Definitely.

So why did her body say otherwise?

Chapter Eight

"I got the expanded, updated trivia pack that goes all the way up to 2020, and I brought a bottle of rosè. It's called M'lady's Blush. It made me think of you." Ray thrust the cards and the bottle at Brynn as he entered the house.

Her place was clean and spacious, a pretty blue split-level with a two-car garage and perfect landscaping. Even though they didn't live more than a few minutes apart, he'd never been in this subdivision before.

It felt like coming home, in a good way, a way he'd never had with Jayla. Brynn took the wine and kissed him, just staying in his arms for a minute. "Smells good in here."

"Rosemary chicken."

"Brynn's hair." He nuzzled her neck and lipped her shoulder.

"The chicken is in the crockpot. The potatoes are already mashed and sitting in a casserole dish."

"Are you tempting me with dessert before dinner, m'lady?" he teased.

"Yes."

"Good." With a grunt, he hooked his arm under her legs, and lifted.

"Ray!"

"I may not make it all the way up the stairs, but I am going to make it *to* the stairs," Ray boasted, swaggering ahead. Brynn wasn't heavy, but her long frame made carrying her a chore of navigation. After he bumped her into several pictures on the wall, Ray reluctantly put her down.

"You're very gallant. Very sweet." Brynn gave him an adoring look that traveled to his cock after stopping off at his heart.

"Not as sweet as you."

***

Ray guessed that some part of his mind believed the first time was a fluke. Or maybe he was waiting for her to call him on the body that wasn't as tight and muscular as it had been in his teens and twenties. He still looked good—good for a dad, right?

Brynn pounced on the queen-sized bed with white and green sheets, ignoring the lights still burning and the sunset fading the light outside the drawn curtains. "Do you want these off?" Ray asked.

"Oh. I guess I thought you might like to— Well, I thought maybe it would be more exciting if—" Brynn trailed off.

"I know I'm dating eye candy," Ray hurried to reassure her.

"Me? Ha! But you... Oh my gosh. I never thought a hot guy would go for me," Brynn confessed, eyeing him hungrily. Especially not someone with abs and that butt, and those tattoos."

"You mean someone with those long, go-on-forever legs, those perfect, bouncy, soft titties, and hair that only angels have? No, I definitely didn't see that coming." Ray hurried to her side and threw caution (and his clothes) to the wind.

"You don't get any extra points for shameless flattery." Brynn tugged his shirt out of his pants and started working on his jeans.

"What about the truth?"

She slid down him with an impish grin, mouth pursed. "You get something else for *that*."

***

Brynn knew her previous sex life hadn't been that great. For one thing, she'd been pregnant, nursing, or post-partum for a good chunk of it, and her husband had been very utilitarian about lovemaking. He had used her to get off, and that was it.

Ray seemed to have an internal checklist he was working through. "What about from behind?"

Doggy style? No. She shook her head.

"Want to try?"

How would she look from behind? Wasn't that kind of... lewd?

"I bet you'll like it." Ray nibbled on her breast and made his way down to her pussy, head bowing in homage.

Brynn shuddered as he started tonguing and massaging her most sensitive pieces. "It couldn't be more naughty than that," she muttered, half-aloud.

"Naughty?" Ray lifted his head slowly, taking her labia with him, pulling it up with a succulent *smack* before releasing her to writhe in pleasure. "Naughty? Like kinky?"

"Yes. No! I don't know. I'm very vanilla."

"Well, I'm very chocolate." He laid his arm next to hers with a smirk.

"You know what I mean."

"Where's that fearless beast who took me to my knees in ten seconds last weekend?" Ray asked.

"The wine helped."

"I don't want you to think you need wine to be comfortable with me. Your body is crazy beautiful. You're delicious. What else is worrying you?"

Brynn thought. That he would push her to do something she wouldn't like? Ray wasn't like that. That it would be embarrassing to be seen in certain positions? Ray didn't think that.

That she was a bad girl?

Well, if she couldn't be a little bit bad by this point in her life, what the hell was she waiting for?

Brynn rolled to her hands and knees, thrusting her hips back. "Take me."

"Yes, ma'am!"

***

"Oh, my God. Ohhhh, oh my God!" Brynn had her head down, ass up. Her fingers were reaching under her stomach, rubbing her clit as Ray pounded her from behind, his thick cock filling every inch of her, making her feel like she was on the edge of exploding and cramping in pleasure at the same time. She felt one hand leave her hip and then return, this time pushing against her puckered anus. "Ray!"

"Shh, I'm not going there, baby. But if I play with the outside, it'll feel really good."

She relaxed out of sheer confusion, and sure enough, the tickling stroke on her backdoor made her pussy clench harder. The daring parts of her brain wondered about taking Ray's big, thick cock in her tight little ass, her pussy full of her own fingers, while her mouth opened in a silent scream of pleasure.

Just the fantasy had her milking his cock to the point where Ray had no choice but to come with her.

"Oh, my God, Brynn. *God.* God, girl, I love you." Ray collapsed against her and pulled her back to his chest.

She swallowed hard. It was just a slip of the tongue, probably. But if he could slip, so could she. "I wanna do everything with you, Ray. I want to try everything with you. I... You're... I trust you. I feel like you're my best friend, and then something else bigger and deeper on top of it," she whispered.

"Let's do it. Let's do it all, Brynn. We didn't make the big time back then, but we're going to make it now. The big life. You and me."

"I don't want anything big and fancy. I want you, and our girls, and our moms. Our town and our students," she half-whimpered as he pulled her to face him.

"Beautiful... Don't you know? That *is* the big time."

Chapter Nine

"What should we do next weekend?" Brynn served the meal in her robe, naked underneath. Part of her wondered if they'd be daring enough to do it on the dining table. Or the kitchen counter. She never had. Of course, she'd have to clean any sexy surfaces afterward. Maybe in the living room, or down in the den of the finished basement?

"Next weekend... I think I want to take my girls out somewhere special."

"Girls? Sammi and Raquel?"

"And you. My favorite girl. Woman. Where is your favorite restaurant?"

"Genoa, the Italian place by the river. My mother takes me there once a year on my birthday. But it's not my birthday and it's expensive," Brynn cautioned.

"Sweetie? Let me spoil you. When was the last time a man did that?"

"Um. The ex. While we were dating. And what about you? You need to be spoiled. Not just in the bedroom," she cut him off as he smirked.

"You do and you will. Brynn? You okay?"

She nodded, then shook her head. "I'm fine. It's just... I don't know. I think I figured the chance to hear those words was gone. Most guys look at me and see a gym teacher who's in her thirties and doesn't have a ring on her finger. They make some assumptions. And then, if they move past those assumptions, they find out that there's a kid in the mix."

"Well, I already know all about crazy teenage daughters. A woman who can do it is a special kind of lady."

"Or man."

"And raising one alone makes you a saint."

"Amen. So," Brynn gave him a brave smile. "I've been waiting for a long time to feel like it was safe to relax and enjoy a man. Enjoy the idea of a man who could fit with me and Sammi. You make me feel like it's safe. A-am I right?" her voice quivered and betrayed her.

Ray looked at her seriously, fork down and eyes locked on hers, the edge of a frown on his handsome face. "Yeah, sweetheart. It's safe."

"No one has called me sweetheart in such a long time."

"Oh yeah? When's the last time somebody called you baby? Or angel? Lover?"

"A long time."

Ray slid into the chair beside hers, lifting her chin until their foreheads touched.

"Will you promise me something, Brynn?"

"Mhm?"

"Promise me you'll let yourself get used to it. I don't want to go anywhere."

***

"I think you can call Mrs. Donovan Brynn when we're out together."

Raquel shifted in her seat, tucking and untucking the bright royal blue dress around her legs. "And Sammi can call you Ray?"

"Yep."

"Are you going to propose at the fancy restaurant?" Raquel demanded suddenly.

Ray almost jerked the car off the road. "What? No! Honey—"

"I wouldn't mind if you did. Like, not this week, but in a little bit. I like her. You know why?" Raquel went back to attacking the hem of her fancy dress.

Ray had a long list of reasons. Brynn was cool. Honest. She respected children. She made wonderful food and spent time with Sammi and Raquel when they visited her house. She had a wicked dunk and yes, they had finally had that game of two-on-two last night.

Another effing tie. It was getting to be a curse.

Or should that be a blessing?

"Why, Rae-Rae?"

"She calls me back. Or texts me. Right away." Raquel's voice shook slightly.

Ray bit his tongue and nodded. He knew that sometime in the past two weeks Raquel had asked if it was okay for her to have Brynn's number, and he'd said okay. It made sense when both of them were taking turns picking up the girls during a week-long community center clinic. This way they could text or call either parent if they needed a ride or the clinic was running long.

"When I text Mom... she gets back to me. She does. But you know... in a couple days. Or hours. Even if I just text good night, sometimes she's on the field, I know. She has to wait until the game is over."

Ray bit his tongue harder. Coaches had their phones on the field. Jayla was the choreographer. Her main role occurred during half-time. It took two seconds to type back goodnight, or even just one of those smiling little sleepy faces. "I'll talk to your mother."

"No, Dad! I get it. We're not... close. But Sammi and her mom are super close. Mrs. Dono—I mean, Brynn—seems like the kind of person who makes time for important people. Of course, it could be an act until she gets you... but then I was thinking about it. You're kind of a dork. You drive a SUV that smells like sweatsocks. You're going to need glasses and go bald in like five years—"

"Raquel Robinson, hush your mouth!"

"You're not rich and famous. You teach *math*." Raquel announced the last part as if it were even more tragic than his imminent baldness (which was not *true*). "So, I don't think it's an act. Neither does Nana. That's pretty convincing."

"I don't know what to say." He really didn't. Ray realized that this was often the case with his baby girl as she turned into an adult. "You know why I like Brynn?" he announced suddenly.

"Why?" Raquel leaned toward him, eyes shining with rabid teen curiosity.

"Because I'll have someone to be confused out of my mind with. Now, stop fussing with your dress, Rae. You look beautiful."

***

"Mom. You know Steve Kingjoy? The guy who works at the community center pool?"

Brynn turned off the engine as they pulled into Genoa's parking lot. She saw Ray's car parked ahead of her. "Steve?" Brynn tried to hide her frown. She didn't like the older teen. He had a tendency to stare at the female patrons of the gym. "Mhm? What about him?"

"You know how Ray picked us up yesterday?"

"Yes?" Her stomach tensed. Sammi wasn't usually the kind to draw out good news, so whatever was coming must not be great.

"Steve asked for my number. And I said no. And he said did I think I was better than him, and I froze up, and-and you know what? All of the sudden, Ray and Raquel were standing behind me, and Ray took Steve by the shoulder and said, 'Let me talk to you for a minute, man.'" Sammi did a great impression of Ray's low, slow voice. "I don't know what he said, but Steve went milkshake white. He didn't bother me today."

"He'd better not! Now, Sammi, you know what to do if a boy bothers you." Brynn took her daughter's hand.

"I know, I know. But," Sammi paused, wrapping her arms around her middle, "it was nice. To feel protected. To feel like I had a dad around. I know my father's not a bad person—but he sure is a bad father."

Brynn winced and nodded, eyes squeezed shut to stop angry tears that sprang too quickly to the surface. "I'm sorry, baby. To tell you the truth, he wasn't much of a husband, either. I married him because I thought I had to."

"It's okay, Mom! I don't miss him. I really don't. But… I think I'd miss Ray if he weren't around. And Raquel and Nana Vi. I know it's just been a month or so, but I like them a lot. I like knowing that if I ever needed a dad-guy, Ray would step up. He's a step-up kinda guy." Sammi turned back to the passenger side mirror and started fixing her hair. "Maybe even a step-dad kinda guy?"

Brynn opened the door and rose on slightly wobbly knees. "We'll see."

***

"I see why you like this place." Ray walked around the terrace, taking in the sight of the river sparkling with the lights appearing on the waterfront as the spring twilight turned to darkness. "The food is amazing and you can walk off dinner before dessert."

Brynn leaned over to him. "Maybe if the girls go to bed quickly after we get home, I can give you a call for some virtual dessert. I figured out how to make video calls from my phone today."

Well. That settled it. "I'd love that. What did you have in mind?" Ray asked, fumbling in the pocket of his navy blue sport coat.

Brynn dipped her head, eyes darting. The girls were a few yards ahead, feeding the ducks in the river. "I don't know. I think you've seen all my best off-court moves, but I'm always up for some plays from my favorite coach."

"Mm, same. Tonight, how about if you try…a little strip tease for me, and just get down to *this*." Ray pressed her hand in his, holding it tight while he worked a stretchy silver bangle over her narrow wrist.

Brynn stepped back and gasped as she held up the charm bracelet. It sparkled in the light, revealing a dangling silver heart and tiny crystal-encrusted basketball. "Oh, Ray! It's beautiful! I love it." Brynn leaned over and kissed his cheek.

"You can do better than that, Mom!" Sammi called.

"Dad, come on! Movie of the week style, let's go!"

Ray shared an eye roll with Brynn. "Teenagers," he grumbled.

"Movie of the week style?" Brynn arched an eyebrow. "Demonstrate, coach?"

Ray whipped her around, bending her back over his arm, and dipping her in a long, smoldering kiss. All around them, restaurant patrons and people strolling the riverbank applauded and whistled. Sammi and Raquel were the most obnoxious of all.

"Get a room, you two!" Raquel called over her thunderous applause.

"Yeah!" Sammi giggled.

Brynn straightened up, still breathless in his arms. "Shall we finish this off-court?"

Ray laughed and pulled her along to their girls. Oh yes. He was looking forward to a lot more off-court action, but as for finishing it? Nope. He was going to keep this game going into endless overtime. He had a feeling his new teammate wouldn't object.

"Come on, ladies. Ice cream on me."

The End

About the Author

Bestselling and award-winning author S.C. Principale believes in writing stories she wants to read, which is why she writes thrillers, mysteries, and steamy paranormal romances. Her stories are filled with strong, sassy heroines and the unique, often otherworldly men who love them. S.C. lives in historic Chester County, Pennsylvania, where haunted battlegrounds serve as never-ending inspiration. S.C. is a self-proclaimed history nerd, following old mysteries, baking, and leading theater and musical groups. Her home life consists of scrounging space for her laptop without tripping over two kids, two dogs, a mischievous chinchilla, and the most patient, sexy husband in the world. **Visit her website for a free gift!**[1]

scprincipaleauthor@gmail.com

Author Website and Newsletter [2]
Twitter[3]
Instagram[4]
Facebook[5]
S.C.'s Sultry Sweethearts Facebook Readers Group[6]
Tiktok[7]

---

1. https://scprincipale.wixsite.com/website

2. https://scprincipale.wixsite.com/website

3. https://twitter.com/SCPrincipale

4. https://www.instagram.com/s.c.principale/

5. https://www.facebook.com/WritesandBites

6. https://www.facebook.com/groups/668289727695362

7. https://www.tiktok.com/@scprincipaleauthor

<u>**Goodreads**</u>[8]
<u>**Amazon**</u> [9]

---

8. https://www.goodreads.com/author/show/14847508.S_C_Principale

9. https://www.amazon.com/S.C.-Principale/e/
   B01FZZL28I%3Fref=dbs_a_mng_rwt_scns_share

Also By S.C. Principale

Paranormal Romance

CrossRealms Universe

<u>CrossRealms: You an' Me Against the World</u>[1]

<u>CrossRealms: Healing Hope</u>[2]

<u>CrossRealms:Gestures</u>[3]

<u>CrossRealms: A Helpful Gentleman</u>[4]

<u>CrossRealms: Wicked Woods</u>[5]

<u>CrossRealms:Shattered</u>[6]

<u>CrossRealms:Mended</u>[7]

<u>CrossRealms: Whole</u>[8]

Pine Ridge Universe

<u>Pale Girl</u>[9]

<u>Mountain Bound: A Monstrous Love Story</u>[10]

<u>Vampire in Vegas: The Complete Trilogy</u>[11]

<u>The Minotaur's Valentine</u>[12]

Pumpkin Spice and Speed Dating

My Name on Your Lips

<u>Haunted Hearts: A Monster Brides Romance</u>[13]

---

1. http://books2read.com/u/bwKrvP

2. http://books2read.com/u/4ApQoK

3. https://books2read.com/u/mlAJJA

4. https://books2read.com/u/3kPnER

5. http://books2read.com/u/m0B8GA

6. https://books2read.com/u/mBwEev

7. https://books2read.com/u/baDAPa

8. https://books2read.com/u/mKpo9d

9. http://books2read.com/u/bPQ0aJ

10. http://books2read.com/u/bPQp6A

11. http://books2read.com/u/3RLqXY

12. https://books2read.com/minotaursvalentine

Stone-Cold Groom: A Monster Brides Romance
B-Deviled: A Monster Brides Romance
Felix Orbus Series
Possessed by the Leonid King[14]
Taken by the Tigerite
Loved by the Leopardine
Saved by the Servali

Forgotten Gods Series
Forgotten Gods: Volume One[15]
Forgotten Gods: Volume Two[16]

Romantic Suspense
Madeline[17]
Passion[18]
Deep Cover
Contemporary Romance
Turning theTables[19]
Repairs[20]
Chocolate Kisses[21]
Chocolate Krinkles and Two Kris Kringles[22]

---

13. https://books2read.com/hauntedheartsmb

14. https://books2read.com/leonidking

15. https://books2read.com/forgottengodsvolumeone

16. https://www.amazon.com/kindle-vella/story/B0BSDMBHMC

17. http://books2read.com/u/mg18BR

18. http://books2read.com/u/3n5DX6

19. http://books2read.com/u/mv1R18

20. http://books2read.com/u/br1oVZ

21. http://books2read.com/u/mg1oYz

<u>**Books and Suits: A Friends-to-Lovers Romance**</u>[23]
<u>**Belgravia Security**</u> [24]
<u>**The Man with the Umbrella**</u>[25]
<u>**Off-Court**</u>[26]
Risky Business in Rovigo
Historical Romance
<u>**Alliance**</u>[27]

---

22. http://books2read.com/u/mVRwkJ

23. http://books2read.com/u/49LMB0

24. https://www.amazon.com/kindle-vella/story/B09DDHWF3C

25. https://books2read.com/themanwiththeumbrella

26. https://books2read.com/offcourt

27. https://www.amazon.com/kindle-vella/story/B0B4F2RB94

Read the next page for an excerpt from
the cozy-but-spicy paranormal romance
The Minotaur's Valentine

The Minotaur's Valentine

S.C. Principale

Milo has finally met the girl of his dreams. She's funny, into 80's metal, loves animals, and wants to be a vet.

And that might come in handy since he's half-bull—a minotaur, to be exact.

But Libby is 100% human and not even aware of the monsters and magic that exist in her new town of Pine Ridge, New York. Everyone tells Milo to be patient and stay in the shadows. Libby's smart and she'll eventually figure out that something's different about this innocent-looking suburb...

Libby Ingersol loves Pine Ridge, but it's lonely being the new girl in town. As another Valentine's Day looms, single Libby is desperate to get out and mingle. When she tries the Pine Ridge club scene, things go wildly wrong.

Can a shy minotaur who wears his heart on his hoof make things go right and salvage Libby's Valentine's night?

The Minotaur's Valentine is a feel-good monster romance with a cinnamon roll hero. Just a warning... cinnamon isn't the only spice you'll find in this happily-ever-after tale of monster love!

Chapter One: Milo

The Night Market is exactly what it says it is. It's a market that's only open at night. It looks like one of those flea markets or farmers' markets that are set up in the civic center parking lot or a school gym during winter break. In the case of the Pine Ridge Night Market, there are about two dozen small stalls set up in the empty lot behind the Pine Loft Coffee Shop. We sell everything from homemade candy and potpourri to weapons for the discerning demon hunter and pre-made potions for nervous spellcasters.

Obviously, you have to know where to look. (And when to look. We're not open every night.)

And humans... humans aren't excluded, especially not humans who've lived in Pine Ridge for a long time, but most won't see the Night Market the way I do.

I don't have specially enhanced vision or anything. No superpowers. I'm just your average, twenty-something minotaur. I put on my jeans one hoof at a time, just like everyone else.

"Milo. Can you fix my watch fob?"

"What's the trouble, Mr. Minegold? Ooh, hey, J.J." I take the watch from the tall, thin, distinguished man wrapped in a black frock coat and bright tartan muffler. His adopted grandson, J.J., is strapped to his hip in one of those stretchy baby-sling contraptions. I look around for something to give the kid, something that won't kill him. I reach under the stall into my big red tackle box and take out several inches of silver chain. "Here you go, little man. Oh!" I draw back at the last second. "It's silver. Can he touch it?"

"Silver doesn't harm Jesse Jakob." Mr. Minegold savors the name, letting his accent become more pronounced as he caresses the curly little head. "Jesse Jakob, you naughty mite! You have tossed off your wooly hat. Your mama and papa won't like that. I must retrace my steps, Milo. I confess I was lingering too long at the fudge stand!"

"I can understand that, Mr. Minegold! I'll look at the watch fob, and you find J.J.'s hat." I wave them off. J.J. waggles his chubby fist, which is now curled around the silver chain.

Dang. Kids are cute. Even human kids. I know J.J. isn't fully human, but he looks human. His dad, Jesse, is a vamp (so is Mr. Minegold), and his mom is... something demon-y? I don't know the details, but she is gorgeous.

My brother, Bill, would tease me if he were still living in town. He'd call me out on my interest in interspecies couples. As soon as Bill turned twenty, he moved back to the family homestead in Greece. He has a beautiful wife and two kids now. He'd also tell me that I'm running out of time to find a girl. I'm almost thirty. Minotaur women like their bulls young, that's what he'd say.

But I don't want to marry a person based on their outer shell, that's what I'd tell him.

And that's how the fight would start. That's how the same dumb argument always starts. And every time, my parents snort and exchange glances and go take their coffee into the kitchen.

I force my focus back to Minegold's watch. I press the fob on the thick, brassy case, careful to keep it pointing at the floor.

Plink.

A thin wooden stake clatters to the cement. It was only a quarter of an inch wide, tipped in silver, and reinforced with an iron core. It *should* have shot out with the force of a small, lightweight missile. "Ahh. The spring action is gone," I mutter, retrieving the stake from where it had landed between my hooves. It was supposed to spring out with a pretty hefty punch so that its razor-sharp tip and inner core (fully encased in wood) would penetrate deep enough to take out a vampire or a werewolf at close range.

Of course, I'm not advocating the killing of *all* vampires and werewolves. The established supernatural community of Pine Ridge is mostly peaceful and dedicated to keeping evil-doers out of our fair little city.

Mr. Minegold, who has been here since the end of World War II, organized a neighborhood patrol long, long ago to drive out or exterminate undesirables. My grandfather came over around the same time as Minegold. But since minotaurs in rural New York have a little trouble blending in, my family has always hung out in the shadows, worked nights, and made friends with other night-dwelling creatures, like Mr. Minegold. He can get around okay in the daytime as long as it's cloudy, but he prefers the night and stays inside during the day whenever he can.

Minotaurs protect. We guarded King Minos' wife and children against his insane rage by taking them into the labyrinth and pledging we would die before they were harmed. Greek history can say what it wants, but minotaurs have always been friends to the weakest among us. In the modern age, that usually means we make the firepower to hunt the *real* monsters.

I slip my headphones (the wireless kind so they don't get tangled around my horns) over my head and cue up Metallica on my phone. "Hey! Mr. Minegold?" I shout down the row of market stalls.

"Yes, Milo?" He turns at once. Vampires have amazing hearing.

"You need a new spring! Twenty bucks and twenty minutes?"

Mr. Minegold beams and waves back, earning smiles and curious looks from the people pushing past him. "You are a godsend! See you in twenty minutes!" He jiggles J.J. on his hip, unearthing a blue knitted cap with a fluffy white pom pom and ear flaps. "Ah! J.J.! There's your hat! Did you have it stuffed in my pocket this whole time? You clever little dumpling!"

My God. Kids are adorable...

I turn up the volume.

Chapter Two: Libby

Have you ever had coffee so good you want to take it back to bed with you? Maybe whisper in its ear and coo a few sweet nothings?

Why, yes. I am single, thank you.

But, that perfectly describes the cinnamon streusel coffee from The Pine Loft Coffee Shop. It was delicious and decadent, sweet and full of warm spices. And cheap. Criminally cheap.

Everything in my new town is ultra affordable. My godmother says that I should consider it a red flag.

"There's nothing cheap about New York, Libby!" Aunt Karen had lectured a few months ago, her thin arms crossed over her bony chest, staring at me with her wild, not-all-there eyes before turning back to her blaring television.

My godmother is a lot like a feral cat, whereas me, I'm a stray. She didn't want to take me in, and I didn't want to stay with her. When she and my mother were best friends back in high school, "Aunt Karen" became my godmother. Then my mom went to work at a daycare where I could come for free, and Aunt Karen moved in with a way-older guy, discovered daytime television, and developed a taste for flavored vodkas. By the time my mom passed away when I was eighteen, Aunt Karen was all alone. Rich, lecherous "Uncle Amir" had been done in by a spectacular cardiac arrest in a strip joint while choking on a cigar and trying to get change from a five out of a neon bikini.

I didn't want to live with Aunt Karen, even sans the not-so-dearly-departed Uncle Amir, so I was a stray. On my own, surviving on scraps of part-time jobs, and a few months of my mother's Social Security benefits before they cut me off.

I went to a cheap college and lived on campus. Antonia College isn't the jewel of the state education system, so they offer perks for coming back each semester, and bonuses when you take summer classes. I had no complaints. I think Antonia is kind of feral, too. It's in the

Endless Mountains of Pennsylvania. It likes to hide from prying eyes, but if you show it a little love, it's decent.

When I graduated with an animal science degree, I found a job as a vet tech. I found a cheap apartment in a cheap town.

Aunt Karen had lectured more when I made my dutiful pilgrimage to see her after graduation. She blew cigarette smoke at her enormous flat screen, obscuring the evil face of a pseudo-psychologist who embarrassed people on television for money. "It's a scam. You'll see."

"It's not a scam. I know people from Pine Ridge. We were buddies in college."

That was a stretch, but Aunt Karen didn't need to know that. When I was a freshman, there was a gorgeous, adorable melanin-challenged couple, Sophie-Something and Jesse-Something Else. They were seniors, and already engaged. Because of the dismal size of Antonia's enrollment, seniors and freshmen were often in the same electives. We ended up in Literature of Ancient Civilization together, sitting in the back row during evening classes. (I worked afternoons at a little taco joint in town.) When we were forced to introduce ourselves during one of the weekly "Pair-and-Share" events the professor had coordinated to discuss Aeschylus and Enheduanna, I told them I was from Allentown, Pennsylvania. It turned out Sophie was from Philadelphia, making us practically neighbors. Jesse was from Pine Ridge, New York, right over the state line.

Sophie and Jesse made his town sound like a dream come true—friendly, little, full of beautiful people and places. They never mentioned how affordable it was, but when you're bored in class and you start looking up random crap on your phone... Well, I couldn't believe my screen.

Sophie and Jesse were planning to get their own place after graduation. They showed me some of the houses they were looking at one night when the antiquated overhead projector overheated and the professor insisted we all sit and wait patiently for it to cool off enough to come back to life.

That's right. I said two college seniors were buying a *house*. At first I figured one of them must've had money, but then a little more talking and a little more squinting at the phone revealed that Pine Ridge real estate seemed to be quite a bargain.

And if they could afford a mortgage, maybe I could afford to rent a room. Or even a whole apartment with a kitchen?

My other option was moving in with Aunt Karen, who had started telling me that I should try to find a "sugar daddy." Uncle Amir 2.0, or a town that sounded too good to be true? I was going to gamble on something that at least sounded like it wouldn't induce vomiting.

Aunt Karen was right there with me on the "too good to be true" part. While I packed the few items I had stashed in her spare room, she trailed after me, wailing in a voice that set off the neighbor's chihuahua. "That little hick town in the mountains sounds too good to be true. You've only been there for a weekend! This is a crazy risk, Lib-Lib. You should move in with me. You don't know *why* it's so cheap! I bet all the babies have birth defects! I bet it's near a nuclear testing site. A sewage station! A slaughterhouse!"

"I stuck around for the summer, Aunt Karen, but I have to go. My lease is signed. My job starts the second week of September. Look, if it's anything like you said, I'll move back. I promise." I may or may not have had my fingers crossed behind my back at the time.

Chapter Three: Libby

Where was I?

Oh, right. Aunt Karen, She-Who-Is-Hysterical. Despite ear-splitting pleas and the arrival of Renaldo or Rudolpho (some swarthy guy with chest hair that resembled roadkill) in his red Boxster, I tore myself away from Allentown and started my new life.

I moved to Pine Ridge in September. It's now January and I haven't seen any babies with two heads, haven't been exposed to sewage or radiation, and the only unreasonable expense is my coffee addiction. The Pine Loft takes a tenth of my paycheck, but I blame that on my own weakness and the fact that I pass the place on my way home from the clinic. I don't get out much, but I think Pine Ridge is perfect.

The only thing that would make it better would be a social life.

Oh, I go out with friends—sort of. It really is a small little town. I asked Dr. Peterson, my boss, if he knew of a couple named Sophie and Jesse, and he did. I looked them up and we've had dinner a few times.

Everyone is friendly, really.

But people seem... guarded or oblivious. Is that mean to say? I don't care, it's true.

There seem to be two kinds of people in this town. Group One includes people who will smile and chat, always super interested in you, but revealing only little, vague basics about themselves. Group Two includes people who smile and chat, talking a ton about themselves, but asking very little about me, the new girl.

I've decided, whether I'm right or not, that this bi-oddity (new word, go me) is because I'm new here. This is a tight-knit town, according to Jesse. (His last name turned out to be Smith.) I figure that people don't want to invest in me too much in case I leave and break their little hearts.

Well, I've got nowhere else to go, so I'm staying.

Sophie, who has only been here a few years longer than me, already seems relaxed. I've seen her in the store showing off their little boy, surrounded by a gaggle of old granny-types, looking like a queen with the heir to the throne.

Jealousy is a bitch.

I'm not jealous of Sophie! I just... I want a family. I want to *fit in*. I've been a loner for a long time, ever since I started realizing that the poor kids on food stamps with single moms don't *quite* fit in, no matter what the teachers said.

So, using the new pastel blue planner my boss had given me for Christmas (stuffed with gift cards to the bookstore, the sushi place, and The Pine Loft), I decided to change that. I had a planner. I was going to plan.

One foggy night last week, with Metallica's *Whiskey in a Jar* blaring as I savored my on-the-way-home cup of coffee, I opened the planner and actually looked at it.

It was pretty straightforward. There were spaces for monthly, weekly, and daily notations. I flipped past the first two weeks of January and discovered a Goals and To-Do Lists section. Dr. Peterson had even left me another present. "Oh, my gosh. I love my boss." Two vinyl sticker collections, both full of metal band logos from the eighties! I would have to ask him where he got such a perfect gift.

But back to the to-do list. I grabbed the matching baby blue gel pen that was stuck through a loop on the side of the planner and wrote:

Have a social life.
Stop living on coffee, cheese puffs, bananas, and sushi.
Find a club.
Get a date.

Chapter Four: Milo

There aren't any other minotaur families in Pine Ridge. The only female minotaur in town is my mother. When we traveled to Greece for my brother's wedding, there were gorgeous girls everywhere. Girl minotaurs, I mean.

I wasn't into them.

After the reception, my dad sat me down on the back of the private yacht my new sister-in-law's family had chartered. My father was a little tipsy. (It takes a LOT of ouzo and champagne to make a minotaur tipsy, in case you're wondering.) He asked me if I was into bulls instead of cows, and I told him no. Then he asked if there was someone back in Pine Ridge that had my heart. I told him no. He asked if I was one of those aromantic types, only he was slurring so it sounded like he asked if I was *aromatic*. After I sniffed at my suit for a few minutes, I told him I didn't smell like I'd bathed in anise, which is what drinking too much ouzo makes you smell like.

By that time, my mom came back on deck, looking for us. My father got this completely unhinged, lustful look in his eyes and started chasing her around the boat.

I was severely tempted to jump overboard and swim ashore.

The truth is, I'm probably one of the most romantic people I know—but no one else knows it.

Minotaurs have a thing for protecting and serving. Acts of service are our love language. I dream about having a wife I can protect and help. She'll look up at me adoringly. She'll be so small next to me that every time I'm around her I'll feel like I'm her living shield, a proud warrior—not just the guy who makes poison rings and recalibrates weaponized watches.

Yes, I said she'd be small next to me. Small and possibly on the helpless side. I admit it. I have a damsel in distress thing, but I'm not some neanderthal brute.

I blame history.

Pull up a chair.

My people were not always called minotaurs. We existed before that whole King Minos crap. We have been around as long as anyone else, human or "monster." Humans feared us, the same way they feared other half-man, half-animals. The peaceable taurosapiens pulled back into the shadows, forming secret rural communities. Every community had an underground lair equipped with escape tunnels and traps to prevent violent humans from attacking the clan.

And then King Minos found out that his wife had become friendly with a local blacksmith (taurosapiens like metal). The way my mother tells it, Pasiphae was nothing more than a friend to the smith, who she had commissioned to make armor for her oldest son, the Prince.

Minos, who was already two hammers short of a forge, decided she was having an affair and went on a murderous rampage, killing one of his own children. My ancestors of course then urged the queen and surviving royal children to take refuge with us.

Well, you know how it is when you're thrown together with someone day after day...

Yeah. Eventually, Pasiphae and Aspro (the smith) were secretly married and had a bunch of little half-human, half-taurosapien babies. And we started being called minotaurs. (I think we should have been called *Pasi*taurs. Why give that murdering idiot any credit? But you can't change two thousand years of history overnight.)

Ever since I saw the picture in mom's old history book, I've been a hopeless romantic. The picture is an old ink illustration that shows Aspro blocking the labyrinth entrance. His eyes are glowing red, his horns are glinting, and his nostrils are flaring. One hand holds a huge broadsword. The other arm is pushing Queen Pasiphae behind him. She's looking up at him with such utter love and adoration.

I want that. I want a woman I would die for and a woman who would be by my side, adoring me as much as I adore her.

That isn't going to happen in Pine Ridge.

There are two kinds of people here. One, there are people who know about the magical energies and entities who live here. They play it cool. They know that everyone isn't what they seem. They're all (99% of them) nice, normal-ish folks. What about the second group?

They are incredibly, stubbornly blind. They walk around with witches, wolves, succubi, and whatever else we have on tap, thinking that everything is normal. According to those people (all human), some of their neighbors are just a bit "eccentric."

The people in the second group would all be dead by dinner time if Pine Ridge weren't such a safe place to live.

Either way, I'm not going to find a woman who needs me here. If she's a vampire, a werewolf, or a witch, she'll be able to take care of herself and probably won't want me being my overprotective self. If she's a normal, oblivious human, she won't ever meet me. If she did, she'd run in terror, and that's no way to start a relationship.

Chapter Five: Milo

The Night Market opens at dusk, but the stall owners who can tolerate sunlight tend to come a little before so they can set up and not waste a single second of selling time.

Stalls are set up in a grid between the light poles in the lot. There are three rows. The ones closest to the street are run by residents who are human or who can pass for human. They also tend to sell stuff human "tourists" would buy, like crystals, fudge, hand-embroidered clothing, and more run-of-the-mill stuff. It's not any kind of "human-looking equals better" mentality, believe me. It was decided a long time ago, back in the fifties when the Night Market was first getting set up, that this arrangement would help the more "unique" vendors stay safe. After all, no matter how oblivious a human is, he or she will notice if you're about seven-feet tall and have horns coming out of your head. My stall is in the back row, the corner spot. It's a prime location.

Christmas, Hanukkah, Yule, Kwanzaa, and Solstice weren't too long ago, so there are still a dozen strands of multi-colored lights strung up between the poles. I think we should leave them up all year. It gives the market a bustling, festive air, and that's important in cold, foggy, mountain towns in January. Festive, fun places attract customers who want to browse. Otherwise, people go straight to the stall they need, buy their potion or bat wings, and get the heck back home to their nice cozy houses.

"Milo! Hey, man!"

"Leo! Good to see you! Back from touring, Mr. Big Shot?"

Leo is a werewolf who is also in a local band. (It's a pretty big deal in the NYC club scene, but he never brags. Actually, he rarely talks at all.) His wife is a witch. They're some of my best customers because they're part of the "Neighborhood Watch." It's not a full moon, so I don't hurry to put my silver-tipped goodies away.

The stocky, auburn-haired man grins at me. "Out again next weekend. We'll be gone for a solid week."

"Ah. Looking for something to fend off those city demons?" I start moving weaponry around, sliding choice pieces forward for Leo to see. Everyone knows violent demons love big cities. Their kills blend in and get blamed on drug dealers and gangs.

"Actually, no. I'm packing Robbie. What else do I need? Plus, Tessa and Charlotte will be with us."

I nod. The two-man band usually travels as a foursome, two sets of best friends, two couples. My heart stabs me in a way I wasn't expecting.

"What can I get you, then?" I ask in a gruff, clipped voice that shocks the hell out of me.

Leo doesn't seem to mind. "Can you make me something pretty?"

I take out one of my tackle boxes. Tackle boxes are great for holding tiny tools and metallic parts like springs and screws. My boxes are covered with all kinds of band stickers. Skin Deep, the band that Leo is in with Robbie, another local (and vampire), has a fair amount of signage on my boxes. Leo sees the stickers and smiles.

"I gotta tip you better," he mutters, hands in his pockets.

"Well, I'd never say no to that." I have a black velvet drape on my table every night. Just because I'm showcasing deadly weapons doesn't mean I can slack on presentation. Right now, I clear a space and put down a selection of poison rings and some of my "daintier" weapons.

Leo looks at a black leather band that has a shiny silver box in the center. From the filigreed box came a knitting-needle thin dagger of shining silver. From the other side was a wooden rod of the same length and thickness with a silver tip.

"Don't trip." My voice is just a rumble in the dark, protective instincts nudging up in my chest. "The silver makes for easy penetration. The wood will slip right through the heart. It'll kill a vamp or a werewolf."

"Hell, that'll kill a human," Leo points out, never losing the half-grin on his face. "Anything in the heart, dude, beating or still. How does it work?" He lightly taps the center of the metal box with its ornate design.

"Telescoping barbs controlled by a catch on the band. It has a safety. The barbs resist pressure, however. An effective weapon that I can demonstrate." I bend down to my insulated lunch box at my feet and pull out a cantaloupe. I'm a vegetarian, and I usually eat one melon per night during my "lunch" break. If I get to use it as a demo first, that's fine. "Let's say this represents a human head."

"Let's say it doesn't. I believe you without puncturing an innocent fruit. How much?"

"Fifty."

"A steal. I'll take it. But can you make me something else, too? Something that isn't a weapon. A necklace?"

I flex my thick fingers, fingers that have a light coating of hair, the same as any bull. These mitts are big, but not clumsy. Still, I wouldn't consider myself adept at jewelry making. I've never really tried it unless it was to conceal a weapon. "There are two other stalls here that sell jewelry, Leo."

"Yeah, and they're both good places, but not what I want. I like your work. Your style. You put something of longing into the metal. Like a little piece of your soul, man."

I blink down at my wares. Really? My soul was in there? Maybe an occasional piece of hair, but... I shrug. Leo is a good customer and he doesn't talk much. That speech contained the most words I've ever heard him say at one time. If it means that much to him, I'll do it. "Sure, Leo. When do you want it and what did you have in mind?"

He hands me a drawing on a creased piece of staff paper. Two interlocking metal hearts, one covered with leaves and flowers, one covered with thorns and spikes. Leo and Tess.

Dang it. My eyes were instantly welling up. The wolf and his witch. My voice cracks, "Two weeks?"

"You're the best, Milo. You know, some woman's going to be so lucky when she finds you."

Leo walks off. I fold the paper carefully and hide it in my tackle box. I feel a tiny sliver of hope in my heart. When Leo speaks, it's important and he means it.

Lucky to find me.

I'll be lucky to find her, too...

Continue reading for an excerpt from
CrossRealms: Healing Hope
by S.C. Principale.

Sometimes two broken people make one whole...

Hope Maguire has always been a loner, both by choice and necessity. She'd learned from a young age not to expect anything from anyone, and that suited her fine. In her line of work, friends would be nothing but liabilities anyway. Most Hunters don't live long, so why get attached? When she's assigned to Malcolm, a stuffy, inexperienced Guardian of the Guild, and then sent to work with the team (ugh!) at the Creek Valley CrossRealms, she's sure it's going to be disastrous.

Self-fulfilling prophecy much?

Approached by a third party and asked to inform on her fellow agents, Hope thinks she's doing the right thing—until it's revealed that she has been a pawn in a deadly double-cross. Now, assassins are after her, and it's run or die. Too bad a near-fatal attack has left her as weak as the prey she used to stalk. Hope knows she is as good as dead. No one will save a Hunter who turned on the good guys. Right?

Malcolm Mansfield-Smythe has always regarded Hunters as tools for killing demons and little else. When his rebellious Hunter betrays them all and then ends up on the chopping block herself, it's tempting to forget about her and keep being the empty, by-the-book man he's always been. Except... he doesn't want to be that hollow automaton anymore, and he doesn't think Hope wants to be a cold-blooded weapon, either. A daring (but poorly planned) rescue leads to a life on the run. Forced to rely only on each other, can two enemies find a way to become friends— or even more?

Healing Hope

Territory

April 2006

"Winters Interventions." Harold Winters picked up the phone at the front desk. Typically, he remained closeted in the back of the agency, but he was currently short-staffed. This investigative agency, which handled paranormal issues as well as the mundane spousal affairs and stolen property, was simply a cover. Oh, his true work dealt with the supernatural as well, but much more intimately.

Harold Winters was a Guardian of the Guild, the secretive and elite group of men and women who possessed the knowledge to train those who could see through the Mists. The Mists cloud most human eyes to the supernatural elements among them.

His receptionist was one such person, and as such, she was out helping on an assignment, tracking down whatever had been terrorizing a rather rundown area of Creek Valley, home of the California CrossRealms, a place where the Heavenly, Earthly, and Hell Realms were separated by only a thin margin.

"It's me," Beryl, the receptionist in question, chirped cheerfully. "Maddox and I killed a big scaly demon by Scarlet's. He was going to ravish me in the back alley, but then he said that might not be a good idea."

"Who, the demon or Maddox?" Winters felt like he had to double-check. His ravishing receptionist was a reverted succubus, after all. Sex was her second nature, a perk for her lucky human fiancee, the stalwart Maddox.

Beryl made a noise of disgust. "Maddox! I'm not into scales. Plus, Celeste and Auggie are here. Also, it's Friday. We haven't had a nice, demon-free evening in weeks. Well, present company excluded."

"I'll pass on the invitation. We *are* rather slammed at the agency, you know." He loved his agents dearly, despite the clear rules that stated Guardians of the Guild should remain firmly detached from them, especially given their startlingly high mortality rate. "I shall stay here and consult with our recently seconded Guardian."

"You two just want to get rid of all the Americans and then drink all the tea and say words like snog and knickers," Beryl huffed. "I don't like Mansfield-Smythe. He's a pompous ass. Not a *lovable* pompous ass like you are. He says Celeste and Auggie shouldn't work together, and Maddox and I can't have sex on my desk. It's *my* desk!"

"Technically it's my desk as I own the premises and all the furnishings, and I happen to agree with him on that point."

"But Maddox says you'd have a stroke if we used *your* desk."

"I am *not* having this conversation."

"I don't like him. He treats us like robots."

Winters pinched the bridge of his nose to stave off the headache he felt surging forth. For a full decade, he'd worked in Guild Headquarters in London. He oversaw a much larger area with many Guardians reporting to him. He regarded all of them with cool, precise detachment. Only a few years in the Creek Valley CrossRealms with a bunch of young upstarts had turned him soft. Oh, he could assist and train his entire team of young Hunters, Warriors, wiccas, and field agents, even associate with the occasional willing Darkling. But five minutes on the phone with Beryl....

She was still talking about Mansfield-Smythe's many faults. "...never goes on field assignments, wants our reports typed and handed in like we're pupils at some freakshow school, never trains in hand-to-hand with us, never even takes his tie off! I think he irons his underwear. And maybe his hair. If you ask me, it's a waste of a cute face and a nice posh accent."

"I did *not* ask you and he's simply doing what other Guardians do, what *most* other Guardians do. *I* am the aberration, not him. Also, he's quite right to recommend that couples do not work in the field together. It can cause distraction and hinder successful missions and investigations."

"You also have way more at stake and you can't let the baddies win. Look, you're old. You have way more experience than he does. This is his first field assignment, right? You teach him! Don't let him corrupt you."

Winters grimaced against the receiver, "My dear, I'm already considered corrupted and irredeemable by most of the Guild. If Felicia hadn't led this team to victory against the dark forces so many times, they'd have stripped me of my rights and titles, my pension and my salary... even my lapel pin."

"Not the sacred lapel pin." Beryl laughed and turned. A strong hand was kneading her shoulder pointedly. "Saving innocent people makes me horny. Maddox, too."

"Dear Lord."

"Just tell everyone who wants to meet at Scarlet's that we'll be waiting for them. In a dark corner behind some potted plants."

Harold Winters hung up, muttering, "Since when does a crowded hole-in-the-wall club like Scarlet's have potted plants? And I'm not old!" He was only forty-two. Mansfield-Smythe was in his late twenties. He supposed that did seem young to Beryl. "Comparatively speaking."

"Winters?" Felicia Montgomery, Winters' surprisingly petite top agent, poked her head in, a strained smile on her face. "There's some girl here. She says she's a new agent."

"What?" Winters practically fell off of his chair. "New— I haven't asked—"

A leggy brunette sidled in behind Felicia, her siren-red tank top and hip-hugging jeans painted onto her curvy body. "You didn't have to ask, Boss Man. I'm just a gift." She smiled seductively at the open-mouthed Guardian. "It's your lucky day, Mal," she purred, sitting on the edge of his cluttered desk.

Harold practically fainted with relief. "Malcolm! There's a... lady here to see you."

May 2006

"You wanna come with us to Scarlet's?" Felicia tried to make their recent addition, a field agent from the New York area, feel welcome. The entire male population of Creek Valley had certainly done their part.

Hope Maguire gave the smaller, sun-kissed blonde a sex-siren smile, her cherry-black lips parting sensually as she tossed her mane of dark hair. "Nah. Got a hot date."

"I'm surprised Mansfield-Smythe lets you off the lead," Nox was slouched in the back, polishing a lethal-looking blade. He never even looked up, or he would have caught the sudden bitterness on Hope's face. It wasn't a dig at the brunette Hunter, but her stick-in-the-bum Guardian.

Both his barb and his refusal to acknowledge her sex-on-legs posturing rankled more than she'd care to admit. No one owned her. And no way in hell she'd want a pasty, pale vampire, even if he was utterly fuckable, those sharp cheekbones, that accent, those eyes.... Nah. Screw it. Her Warrior senses went haywire whenever she was around him.

"Shut up, Nox. Winters paid you. To use the British slang you love to ruin my ears with, 'shove off.'" Felicia sent a withering glare at the Darkling turned informant-turned-occasional-backup.

No one needed to notice that the glare lingered, meeting his piercing blue eyes for a little too long.

Hope felt a whip crack in the middle of her spine. It was true. What the Rogues said was true.

Nox lifted his head, nostrils flared. Fear? Sex? Adrenaline? He kept his eyes on Felicia. "I'm not invited to Scarlet's, Huntress?"

"You're only here so I don't kill you and because we can't handle Guild business and Winters Interventions business at the same time. Someone must be brewing something." Felicia tore her eyes from his with an effort.

"Yes, so much so that you have to bring in the hired muscle and the slut bomb," Nox chuckled darkly. "And Guardian-the-Younger."

Hope, AKA the slut bomb, drew a stake from her waistband as casually as most would check their phones. "Well, since the slut and the Guardian are here, it seems like they don't need you anymore. I'll just save Winters some money." *And put a stop to what's brewing... Little Miss Innocent can't see the Big Bad Wolf wants to take a bite out of her.*

"Don't!" Felicia pulled Hope's elbow sharply.

"What's wrong, Valley Girl? I'll get you another vamp. One who knows his place." Hope shrugged the smaller woman's arm off, never losing her smile.

"I don't want another vampire! I don't want this one." Felicia felt truth wriggling in the back of her brain. She and Nox weren't friends or anything, but they had a mutual truce. They helped each other. Sometimes... sometimes she thought it might be worth giving her heart to someone again, or at least letting it out of its cage.

"You already had one vamp. That's what everyone says."

"Liam's a decent vampire. He has his human soul. He works for the Guild."

"Ooh, freaky girl." Hope cocked her head appraisingly. "I've heard some Warriors get off on it. The risk. The rush. Maybe I *should* try it myself." Her eyes lingered over Nox's taut body, rising slowly, blade resting on the bench at his back.

"Leave her alone," Nox said in a flat voice, resisting the urge to let his fangs slide free.

Hope's eyes traveled between Felicia and the vampire. Nox didn't have a soul, but he didn't kill. He had some "truce" with Winters and his privileged little pets. All of them were so cuddly close to one another, all "Besties" and "Bros." All bonded. Practically inbred.

Throw in the vampire.

Corruption. Contamination.

"Awww, look at that," Hope breathed. "Got yourself a pet, Montgomery? Is he a good little lapdog? Or more of a pussy?"

A lot of things happened at once. Nox lunged and growled, Hope's stake was raised again, and Felicia jumped in the middle.

"Stop! Nox helps us, he doesn't hurt anyone!" Felicia's fingers locked on Hope's elbows, forcing her raised arms to her sides.

"Mind your mouth," Nox snarled at the struggling brunette.

"I'm surprised she doesn't mind yours. You like the bites, Blondie?" Hope knew she was burning bridges. She didn't care. The Rogues would be in charge soon enough.

There was a crack and a snap. Felicia broke the stake in her bare hand, her Warrior strength on full display. "What the hell is wrong with you?"

"I was just going to ask you the same question. I'm outta here. I'll pass on the drinks. I'm not really into the red stuff," she panted, humiliated. That short little blonde couldn't necessarily beat her, but she could force her to a draw. Hope stormed out.

She was done with those losers.

***

"You were right. You guys were so right. They've crossed the line, all of them." Hope paced the gray box-like room.

"The first vampire was a warning. That the Guild ever accepted Montgomery's lover, even with his human soul restored... They wouldn't have if she and Winters weren't so influential. You see how that ended."

"Hot vampires. It's like the gateway drug, man." Hope chuckled grimly.

The shadowy figure continued. "Then the succubi. The witches. There's another vampire among them now, not a soul in sight. He killed several Heaven Fallen in the past, you know."

Hope didn't know, but she nodded as if she did. She never let anyone see a weakness, even a tiny one like ignorance of a simple fact. She'd had a Guardian once. Nice lady. Prim and annoying, rattling on about Mists and magics. She ignored most of it, except for the parts about monsters. She vaguely remembered hearing about Heaven Fallens, too, Warriors and Hunters that had died in battle and been returned to earth with extra powers, way beyond what normal Hunters and Warriors had. So Nox had killed some of them? More to the vamp than she'd thought.

"Nox is more than just an informant from what I've heard. He's bedding Winters' team leader?"

"Miss Perfect? Yeah," Hope lied again, comfortable with lies, far more than the truth. In the weeks that she'd come to be around the little group of agents, she'd come to hate them all. They all... pretended they weren't hurting. They were okay and happy, one big Partridge Family with a side of the undead. Felicia was the worst, a Warrior like her. Blondie clearly wanted to bond... but there was nothing they could bond over. Felicia was living a lie. Warriors and agents don't have friends. They don't have families. They don't have careers and dreams. Felicia still went home to Sunday dinner with her mother, for fuck's sake! She went to college. College.

Like a real girl. Normal girl.

"Maguire, if you don't want this chance, I have a dozen agents more experienced and willing. Let's not forget that you failed to keep your last Guardian alive." The man in the shadows spoke, leaning forward to reveal gray stubble and pulled tight over long jaws.

Hope swallowed hard. That was a low blow, but she deserved it. Her Guardian had been the first one to believe she wasn't some psycho chick, some drug-whore, seeing monsters. She helped Hope to get out of the last mental health facility the state had put her in. They worked together for a little over three months before a demon ripped the middle-aged Guardian in half, right before Hope's horrified eyes.

She was only nineteen when it happened.

She was twenty now, a lifetime in months, barely a year, turning harder than she already was.

I'm an effing diamond.

"I want this chance. Tell me what to do. I'll put that vamp in the ground, you know I can. I've killed—"

"I know you've killed many demons in your short time as a Warrior." The man rose. "I'm sure the Guild has been appropriately grateful?"

Hope hesitated. She ran after her Guardian's body hit the ground, unable to look at the two halves, still twitching. Abandoning her post and turning to her more familiar lifestyle of running, taking, and stealing for survival, the Guild had paid her nothing for the better part of a year. She would have a few weeks' pay soon, now that she'd reluctantly reported to the cardboard cutout, Mansfield-Smythe.

"They're grateful enough," Hope shrugged.

"But we are more so. We are exceedingly grateful to have you as our ally. We can pay you handsomely, take care of you as you deserve to be cared for, an asset, not merely an accessory."

Honeyed words, spoken in a factual voice, a tiny current of the trans-Atlantic running through it. Winters and Mansfield-Smythe had enough toys in their sandbox. She was a lone wolf, meant to stand out. Meant to be feared.

"I'll do it. Anything you say."

"Welcome to the Rogues." The man extended his hand, the rest of his body still bathed in shadow, a key in his palm. "I believe you'll enjoy your new accommodations, a luxury flat. Far better than the slum you've been bunking in."

Hope's cheeks flushed. They knew where she was staying? "Sounds good. What do I call you?"

"Sir."

He rattled her. She never showed that. "Oooh. I could dig it. Strong, silent... shadowy. Strong hands. Strong other things?" Maybe a little spanking, a little choking, a lot of hair-pulling.... She was tired of men who couldn't keep up. She'd guess from his voice that he was in his late fifties, early sixties, way too old for her tastes, but her tastes hadn't always mattered when she needed to trade favors. Powerful, though. Obviously powerful. She liked taking the powerful men to their knees, even if they made her get on hers first. "Why don't you come over here, Baby, and show me?" Sex was a good way to keep them off-balance, too. They thought they were the predators, but oh no. These days, men were always her prey.

"Stop. That sort of talk is detrimental to the cause. There will be no fraternization." The man's voice rang with contempt.

"Sorry. Sir." She hated that word. Both words, actually. Sorry was a word for losers. Well, losers who would admit they were losers. "What's my assignment, Sir? I've infiltrated. Informed."

"You've burnt your bridges there, Maguire. They'll never welcome you back into the fold now."

Hope felt a shiver run through her sinuous body, not the erotic kind she liked. As much as she hated them, Montgomery and her little crew had tried. Mansfield-Smythe was a prick, but he never hurt her. Aside from the demons, they were good people. Even the demons were pretty harmless.

She could never admit mistakes. Back to that weakness thing. Hope waited in silence for the man to answer her question.

"Winters is being controlled and corrupted. Whether he is aware or not, we can see what's happening, not with that foolish demon-worshipping witchcraft, but with pure science. The energy disturbances are worsening considerably. Soon there will be a Realm Rift, if not a full tear, a total breach. Winters and his team are no longer fit to safeguard this CrossRealms. The Guild itself is not fit. They've been hoodwinked into believing that association with Darklings can be tolerated. It cannot. If they're not stopped, we may lose Creek Valley to the Hell Realm."

Hope swallowed. "That would suck."

He ignored her attempt at understatement. "It's time for new blood to control our efforts in the Mortal Realm. The Guardians are stagnated and weak, misaligned." The English accent grew more pronounced. So did the glint of madness in the gray-blue eyes. "The Rogues must control the California CrossRealms, or we may lose this town, then the state. Demons will flood the realm and spread. We must not be stopped by half-efforts."

"Yes, sir." This sounded like action. Hardcore, the war is on, guns-a-blazing action. The shiver returned, this time moving lower, resting between her hips.

"Winters' agents are too loyal to him to turn him over to the Guild or to stand down for the Rogues."

"Yeah, I've seen that. It's sick. He's Daddy Dearest to all of them. And that snotty twerp, Mansfield-Smythe, is bad news in a whole different way."

"Precisely. He'll be recalled soon."

"He will?" Hope frowned briefly. How did this guy know the Guild's plans for their prim and proper Poster Boy?

"It's customary to recall the Guardians of a post for debriefing after a tragedy. Once we're in charge, he'll have no need to return"

"What? What tragedy?" Hope shook her head. Had she lost the thread? They were going to prevent the tragedy before it could happen. She hated being called a hero or anything sappy like that, but that was kind of her deal— even if she was pretty bad at it.

"The death of Mr. Harold Winters. I expect him to be removed within the week. I'd appreciate it if you could take out the blonde bitch, too. The wiccas, as well. The succubus and the vampire are a matter of course. The rest are of little consequence."

"But... Winters is a human." Hope cocked her head, stomach churning.

"And?"

"And... I...."

"I don't have time for him to die a natural death. And of course, since you know my desires, I'm afraid I can't really wait for you to die a natural death, either."

Hope jumped at the unmistakable click of a safety going off. "I'll do it."

"Excellent." The man let her see a cold smile for a split second. "Then, when I appoint a new Guardian, I shall place you as his chief agent."

"Guardian?" She cocked her head.

He waved away the slip of a tongue impatiently. "For want of a better term. A Rogue Commander. Now, go. Don't try to contact me. I will contact you. After all," he handed her a piece of paper with an address typed on it, "I know where you live."